Biography Today

Profiles of People of Interest to Young Readers

Sports Series

Volume 8

Cherie D. Abbey
Managing Editor

615 Griswold Street • Detroit, Michigan 48226

Cherie D. Abbey, *Managing Editor*
Kevin Hillstrom and Laurie Hillstrom, *Staff Writers*
Barry Puckett, *Research Associate*
Allison A. Beckett and Linda Strand, *Research Assistants*

Omnigraphics, Inc.

* * *

Matthew P. Barbour, *Senior Vice President*
Kay Gill, *Vice President — Directories*
Kevin Hayes, *Operations Manager*
Leif Gruenberg, *Development Manager*
David P. Bianco, *Marketing Consultant*

* * *

Peter E. Ruffner, *Publisher*
Frederick G. Ruffner, Jr., *Chairman*

The information in this publication was compiled from the sources cited and from other sources considered reliable. While every possible effort has been made to ensure reliability, the publisher will not assume liability for damages caused by inaccuracies in the data, and makes no warranty, express or implied, on the accuracy of the information contained herein.

This book is printed on acid-free paper meeting the ANSI Z39.48 Standard. The infinity symbol that appears above indicates that the paper in this book meets that standard.

Printed in the United States

Contents

Preface

Welcome to the eighth volume of the **Biography Today Sports Series**. We are publishing this series in response to suggestions from our readers, who want more coverage of more people in *Biography Today*. Several volumes, covering **Artists, Authors, Scientists and Inventors, Sports Figures, and World Leaders,** have appeared thus far in the Subject Series. Each of these hardcover volumes is 200 pages in length and covers approximately 10 individuals of interest to readers ages 9 and above. The length and format of the entries are like those found in the regular issues of *Biography Today*, but there is **no duplication** between the regular series and the special subject volumes.

Volume Eight Devoted to Olympic Athletes

The 2002 Olympic Winter Games, held in Salt Lake City, Utah, were an exciting series of sporting events that showcased some of the best athletic talent in the world. That's why this special volume in our **Biography Today Sport Series** is devoted to Olympic athletes. The 2002 Olympics provided a wide range of sports, from ice hockey (Cammi Granato) to skiing (Simon Ammann, Shannon Bahrke, Jonny Mosely), to snowboarding (Kelly Clark, Chris Klug), and much more. The 2002 Olympics featured the first time that skeleton was included as a medal sport (Jim Shea, Jr.) and also featured the first black athlete ever to win a gold medal at the Winter Olympics (Vonetta Flowers, for bobsled). Above all, the Winter Olympics showcased the determination, sacrifice, and hard work it takes to become a great athlete. We know you'll enjoy their stories.

The Plan of the Work

As with the regular issues of *Biography Today*, this special subject volume on **Sports** was especially created to appeal to young readers in a format they can enjoy reading and readily understand. Each volume contains alphabetically arranged sketches. Each entry provides at least one picture of the individual profiled, and bold-faced rubrics lead the reader to information on birth, youth, early memories, education, first jobs, marriage and family, career highlights, memorable experiences, hobbies, and honors and awards. Each of the entries ends with a list of easily accessible sources designed to lead the student to further reading on the individual and a current address. Obituary entries are also included, written to provide a perspective on the individual's entire career. Obituaries are clearly marked in both the table of contents and at the beginning of the entry.

Biographies are prepared by Omnigraphics editors after extensive research, utilizing the most current materials available. Those sources that are generally available to students appear in the list of further reading at the end of the sketch.

Indexes

A new index now appears in all *Biography Today* publications. In an effort to make the index easier to use, we have combined the **Name** and **General Index** into one, called the **Cumulative Index**. This new index contains the names of all individuals who have appeared in *Biography Today* since the series began. The names appear in bold faced type, followed by the issue in which they appeared. The Cumulative Index also contains the occupations, nationalities, and ethnic and minority origins of individuals profiled. The Cumulative Index is cumulative, including references to all individuals who have appeared in the *Biography Today* General Series and the *Biography Today* Special Subject volumes since the series began in 1992.

The Birthday Index and Places of Birth Index will continue to appear in all Special Subject volumes.

Our Advisors

This series was reviewed by an Advisory Board comprised of librarians, children's literature specialists, and reading instructors to ensure that the concept of this publication — to provide a readable and accessible biographical magazine for young readers — was on target. They evaluated the title as it developed, and their suggestions have proved invaluable. Any errors, however, are ours alone. We'd like to list the Advisory Board members, and to thank them for their efforts.

Sandra Arden, *Retired*
Assistant Director
Troy Public Library, Troy, MI

Gail Beaver
University of Michigan School of Information
Ann Arbor, MI

Marilyn Bethel, *Retired*
Broward County Public Library System
Fort Lauderdale, FL

Nancy Bryant
Brookside School Library,
Cranbrook Educational Community
Bloomfield Hills, MI

Cindy Cares
Southfield Public Library
Southfield, MI

Linda Carpino
Detroit Public Library
Detroit, MI

Carol Doll
Wayne State University Library and Information Science Program
Detroit, MI

Helen Gregory
Grosse Pointe Public Library
Grosse Pointe, MI

Our Advisory Board stressed to us that we should not shy away from controversial or unconventional people in our profiles, and we have tried to follow their advice. The Advisory Board also mentioned that the sketches might be useful in reluctant reader and adult literacy programs, and we would value any comments librarians might have about the suitability of our magazine for those purposes.

Your Comments Are Welcome

Our goal is to be accurate and up-to-date, to give young readers information they can learn from and enjoy. Now we want to know what you think. Take a look at this issue of *Biography Today*, on approval. Write or call me with your comments. We want to provide an excellent source of biographical information for young people. Let us know how you think we're doing.

Cherie Abbey
Managing Editor, *Biography Today*
Omnigraphics, Inc.
615 Griswold Street
Detroit, MI 48226
www.omnigraphics.com

Simon Ammann 1981-

Swiss Ski Jumper
Winner of Two Gold Medals in Men's Ski Jumping at
the 2002 Winter Olympics

BIRTH

Simon (pronounced *SEE-mon*) Ammann was born on June
26, 1981, to Henrich and Margrit Ammann. He was raised in
Unterwasser, a mountain village in the Toggenburg Valley in
eastern Switzerland. Ammann, whose nickname is "Simi,"
has four siblings.

YOUTH AND EDUCATION

Ammann grew up in Switzerland, a mountainous country in northern Europe that provides all sorts of opportunities for winter sports activities. Bobsledding, skiing, snowshoeing, camping, mountain climbing, and hiking are all very popular with the Swiss people. As a youngster, Ammann was able to enjoy many of these outdoor sports. His hometown of Unterwasser is surrounded by beautiful mountains, and he and his friends often swished down their steep slopes on skis.

When asked to discuss his dramatic improvement in 2001, Ammann explained that he had learned to balance athletics and academics. "It is also a result of better training, in particular muscle training which has helped strengthen me up, and the excellent help from all the Swiss team."

Ammann became involved in the sport of ski jumping when he was only nine years old. At the top levels of ski jumping, athletes soar off a long downhill ramp into the air, flying the length of two football fields before landing. During their flight, they lean forward and keep their bodies parallel to their skis, which they position into a V shape. At the end of the flight, the skiers use their knees and hips to absorb the shock of the landing. Competitors earn points based on the distance they travel and their form during flight and landing.

During his first few years of ski jumping, Ammann failed to come anywhere close to the distances posted by professional skiers. But after a few years of practice, it was clear that he possessed all of the qualities necessary to become one of the country's top ski jumpers, including athletic ability, boldness, and an instinctive understanding of the aerodynamics of flight and the ways in which wind and velocity can influence a jump. By his mid-teens, Ammann had improved so much that he was regularly competing in both 90-meter and 120-meter ski jumping events all around Europe.

Ammann attended school in Unterwasser throughout this period. But balancing the demands of schoolwork and training was difficult. For example, the young teen often traveled to foreign countries to practice his jumps since no 120-meter courses existed in Switzerland. As a result, Ammann completed many of his homework assignments during train or automobile rides to and from distant places.

CAREER HIGHLIGHTS

Throughout his teenage years, Ammann ranked as one of the smallest ski jumpers in the world. Even at age 20 he stood only five feet, eight inches tall and weighed no more than 120 pounds. But he was able to use his mastery of ski jumping technique and his adventurous nature to climb up through the ranks of Switzerland's skiers. By 1998 he had honed his skills to the point that he qualified to compete in the Winter Olympic Games at Nagano, Japan.

The 1998 Winter Olympics

When Ammann arrived at Nagano, he was not among the world's top ski jumpers. He competed there in two events: the 90-meter jump (also known as the low hill jump) and the 120-meter jump (the high hill jump). He managed only a 35th place finish in the 90-meter event and a 39th place finish in the 120-meter event. Nonetheless, he enjoyed immensely the experience of representing his country in Olympic competition. By the time he returned home to Unterwasser, he was already dreaming about flying through the air at the 2002 Winter Games in Salt Lake City, Utah.

In the late 1990s Ammann continued to compete on the World Cup ski jumping circuit—the premier ski jumping competitions in the world. But he posted several mediocre seasons on the circuit. In fact, he became better known for his resemblance to J.K. Rowling's fictional Harry Potter character than for his ski jumping exploits. As the 2001-2002 season progressed, however, Ammann seemed poised to take his performances to a higher level. First, he qualified for a spot on the Swiss team for the 2002 Winter Olympics. In addition, he earned two second places and two third places in World Cup events in December 2001 alone. When asked to discuss his dramatic improvement, Ammann explained that he had finally learned to balance his ski jumping training with his academic studies. "It is also a result of better training, in particular muscle training which has helped strengthen me up, and the excellent help from all the Swiss team," he said.

In January 2002, however, Ammann suffered a big crash during a practice run on a course in Germany. The young skier later tried to downplay the seriousness of the injury. "It looked spectacular landing on my neck and head, but it wasn't actually that bad," he said. "I had a few bruises and scratches on my face, so I took a few days off but then I continued training again." In reality, however, the crash landing also gave Ammann a concussion and forced him to sit out several events on the World Cup tour.

Ammann competing during the 90-meter men's ski jump at the 2002 Olympics.

The 2002 Winter Olympics

In February 2002 Ammann and the rest of the Swiss team arrived at the Winter Olympic Games in Salt Lake City, Utah, ready to compete against other athletes from around the world. His first event was the 90-meter hill, which had been dominated by Germany's Sven Hannawald and Poland's Adam Malysz in recent years. In fact, Hannawald and Malysz had been dominating the international ski jumping circuit in both the 90-meter and 120-meter events for the past several years.

Nearly every expert, skier, and ski jumping fan believed that the gold medal winner in the 90-meter event would be either Hannawald or Malysz. Certainly, no one considered Ammann to be a gold medal prospect. After all, he had never won an international competition in his career. For his part, Ammann approached the event with a confident but realistic attitude. "I felt I could be among the top people," he recalled. "But I didn't imagine it would be possible to win."

An Inspiring Performance

As Ammann waited to make the first of his two runs on the 90-meter course, he admitted that he felt "horrible, I was so nervous." But when his turn came, he turned in a nearly flawless 98-meter jump that put him in the hunt for the gold medal along with Malysz and Hannawald. Ammann then completed a terrific 98.5-meter leap with a perfect landing on his second jump. He pumped his fists in triumph after his skis hit the snow, for he knew that he had probably earned a medal. "Ski jumpers know right away whether it's a good jump or not—it's very soon after takeoff

"Ski jumpers know right away whether it's a good jump or not—it's very soon after takeoff when you know. Of course, I knew it was a good jump, and I started to wonder what it would feel like if I won. Then I started to worry, 'What if I didn't win?'"

when you know," Ammann recalled. "Of course, I knew it was a good jump, and I started to wonder what it would feel like if I won. Then I started to worry, 'What if I didn't win?'"

After completing his second jump, Ammann waited anxiously for the official results at the bottom of the hill with his Swiss teammates. "I was sure he had a medal, but I wasn't sure it was gold," said one teammate. "He was quite calm. You could feel he was strong." The scoreboard then flashed the results, showing that Ammann had come out of nowhere to claim the gold medal for Switzerland. He had finished at the top of the leader board with 269 points, while Hannawald had been forced to settle for a silver medal with a score of 267.5 points. Ammann was instantly mobbed by teammates who first pinned the slender young man to the ground, then hoisted him to their shoulders in triumph. Competitors from other countries also expressed delight with his stunning victory. "I can't believe that he put it together like that," said American ski jumper Alan Alborn. "That's great. It was kind of boring to see the same guys winning all the time."

Ammann confessed that he was shocked to win a gold medal. "I am normally much better on the big hill, so winning on the 90-meter hill was obviously a big surprise," he explained. "My goal was to finish in the top 10. I knew it would be difficult against this very advanced field. I needed some luck. But it wasn't only luck but skill as well. I was jumping good enough to become Olympic champion. It is a little surprising."

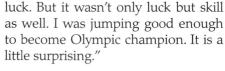

> *Ammann confessed that he was shocked to win a gold medal in the 90-meter event. "I am normally much better on the big hill, so winning on the 90-meter hill was obviously a big surprise. My goal was to finish in the top 10. I knew it would be difficult against this very advanced field. I needed some luck. But it wasn't only luck but skill as well. I was jumping good enough to become Olympic champion. It is a little surprising."*

Meanwhile, television, radio, and newspaper reporters rushed to produce stories about the young Swiss ski jumper. They were drawn to Ammann not only because of his achievement, which gave Switzerland's its first skiing medal in the Olympics since 1972, but also because of his Harry Potter-like appearance. "I can't deny we do resemble each other a bit," Ammann said. "But I promise you there were no fairies weaving their wands over me on that hill." He also admitted that he enjoyed the attention, although he added that he felt a little bit frazzled by all the fuss. "Today has been a marathon of stress," he admitted.

Ammann treasured every aspect of the medal ceremony for the 90-meter ski jumping event, from the playing of the Swiss national anthem to the moment when the gold medal was placed around his neck. He later admitted that he did not want to see the ceremony end. But despite his happiness and satisfaction, he knew that he had another event for which he needed to prepare.

Winning a Second Gold Medal

Three days after the 90-meter event concluded, Ammann, Malysz, Hannawald, and the other ski jumpers gathered together for the 120-meter ski jump. As Ammann readied himself for his first run, he looked down on

Ammann in the Olympic trials for the 120-meter men's ski jump.

the huge throng of spectators—more than 20,000 fans by some estimates —with a new level of confidence. After all, he already had one gold medal under his belt, and the 120-meter jump was his best event.

Amman easily advanced to the medal round of the competition. He then unveiled an excellent jump and landing on the first of his two runs down the course. This effort enabled him to secure a tie for first place with Hannawald after the first round of jumps was completed. Since Ammann and

Hannawald were tied for first at the mid-point of the event, they were the last athletes to make their second jumps. Ammann went first. He streaked down the ramp and sailed out into the air like an arrow. After completing a long, graceful jump, he nailed the landing to keep his place at the top of the leader board. This performance placed all the pressure on Hannawald, the last jumper in the competition. If he executed a great jump, he might be able to wrest the gold away from Ammann. Otherwise, the young Swiss sensation would be able to claim a second Olympic gold medal.

Ammann's amazing triumph set off a whole new round of celebration and excitement within the Swiss Olympic team. After all, his two gold medals equaled the total number of medals of any kind won by the entire Swiss team in the 1998 Olympics. "I am trembling. There are no words for this. I was so nervous. After takeoff, I was flying away. I felt this jump was really, really good. I can't believe it. I am the champion."

On Hannawald's second and final attempt, he delivered a tremendous jump that delivered him far down the hill. But his hand touched the ground when he landed, resulting in deductions from his score. These deductions pushed the German skier down to fourth place and enabled Ammann to clinch gold for a second time. Polish skier Adam Malysz claimed silver and Matti Hautamaeki of Finland earned the bronze to round out the medal winners in the event.

Ammann's amazing triumph set off a whole new round of celebration and excitement within the Swiss Olympic team. After all, his two gold medals equaled the total number of medals *of any kind* won by the entire Swiss team in the 1998 Olympics. "I am trembling," Ammann admitted afterward. "There are no words for this. I was so nervous. After takeoff, I was flying away. I felt this jump was really, really good. I can't believe it. I am the champion."

Amman's second gold medal performance also prompted another wave of media coverage. He sat down for countless interviews and received invitations to appear on the Jay Leno and David Letterman late night television programs. "It was unexpected, and I suppose it does feel like I'm in a dream," he admitted. Underneath all the media talk about his Harry Potter-like appearance, though, most television and magazine coverage em-

*Ammann smiles after his gold-medal winning jump in the
120-meter event at the 2002 Olympics.*

phasized that Ammann symbolized the purity of the Olympics at their best. "If you missed all the rest and saw only the kid from Switzerland soaring into the Olympic history books, and then blinking and flapping his arms to convince himself that it was real, you saw enough to make the 2002 Olympics indelible [unforgettable]," wrote Jim Klobuchar in the *Christian Science Monitor*. "Sometimes it's good to remind ourselves that these are not, after all, super men and women. They are human beings of remarkable skills and strength but frailer than most emotionally—because of their huge commitment of ego and ambition, and because the competition at their level of performance is so relentless. When you're tempted to forget that, a Simon Ammann emerges to restore the Olympics, just momentarily, to the innocence and the ideal that it lost somewhere between billion-dollar budgets and the old olive groves of Greece a few thousand years ago."

Ammann states that "having success is really cool. The only thing I regret, of being so popular now, is that I can't go unknown to a disco and go dancing and acting totally crazy till early in the morning, like I love to do. But I guess that is a part of my success. I can switch between being totally focused on the sport and having fun and letting loose."

A Hero's Welcome

Ammann returned home to Switzerland on February 24. When he arrived at the airport in Zurich, he was shocked to see thousands of cheering fans waiting for him. "That's awesome, unbelievable!" he said when he saw the crowd. "I can't believe it, that this, everything, is just for me. They treat me like a king, but I absolutely don't feel like one. I just did what I love the most: ski jumping. I never expected to win two gold medals at the Olympics, especially not after my last three seasons, which were absolutely terrible. But since I started with ski jumping, I always dreamed about becoming world or Olympic champion, and deep inside, I always knew that I could make it one day. I just didn't expect it so soon."

As Ammann progressed down the road to Unterwasser, he saw banners and flags bearing his name displayed all along the route. After arriving in town he held a joyful reunion with his family and friends, then prepared for a full day of festivities in his honor. The townspeople held a parade in his honor, carrying him through town in a horse-drawn carriage. The young skier also received an amazing assortment of gifts, ranging from a new automobile to a live pig that was said to be a good luck charm. "You know, it's absolutely amazing what the people here do for me," he said.

Ammann's coaches believe that he has a bright future ahead of him. They think that his maturity will allow him to keep his fame in perspective. "He has shown here how he can concentrate on his sport, but also enjoy the atmosphere with people around him," said Coach Berni Scholdler. "Hopefully, this is the start of something great for Simi and for the sports in Switzerland." For his part, Ammann states that "having success is really cool. The only thing I regret, of being so popular now, is that I can't go unknown to a disco and go dancing and acting totally crazy till early in the morning, like I love to do. But I guess that is a part of my success. I can switch between being totally focused on the sport and having fun and letting loose."

Indeed, by the time the 2001-2002 World Cup season drew to a close, Ammann had proven that he intends to remain a force in international ski jumping competitions for some years to come. He rose to seventh place in the circuit's overall standings, and on March 17, 2002, he recorded his first ever World Cup victory.

HOME AND FAMILY

Ammann lives at home with his parents in Unterwasser. He says that he has a girlfriend, but prefers to keep his romantic life private.

HOBBIES AND OTHER INTERESTS

In addition to skiing, Ammann enjoys skating, volleyball, and mountain biking. He is also a big fan of German fantasy author Wolfgang Hohlbein.

HONORS AND AWARDS

Olympic Ski Jumping, 90-meter: 2002, Gold Medal
Olympic Ski Jumping, 120-meter: 2002, Gold Medal

FURTHER READING

Periodicals

Baltimore Sun, Feb. 14, 2002, p.D8
Christian Science Monitor, Feb. 15, 2002, Section USA, p.1
Columbus (Ohio) Dispatch, Feb. 14, 2002, p.D1
Denver Post, Feb. 11, 2002, p.C3; Feb. 19, 2002, p.D8
New York Times, Feb. 14, 2002, p.D1; Mar. 2, 2002, p.D5
Philadelphia Inquirer, Feb. 11, 2002, p.E10
San Francisco Chronicle, Feb. 14, 2002, p.C1
Seattle Times, Feb. 11, 2002, p.D8; Feb. 14, 2002, p.D7
Time International, Feb. 25, 2002, p.49

USA Today, Feb. 11, 2002, p.D10; Feb. 14, 2002, p.D6
Washington Post, Feb. 11, 2002, p.D16; Feb. 18, 2002, p.D14

Online Articles

http://news.bbc.co.uk/winterolympics2002/hi/english/other_skiing/
  newsid_1821000/1821584.stm (*BBC News,* "Swiss Harry Potter Takes
  Flight," Feb. 15, 2002)
http://detnews.com/2002/olympics/0202/11/sports-413308.htm
  (*DetroitNews.com,* "Switzerland's Ammann Surprises the Competition,"
  Feb. 11, 2002)

ADDRESS

Simon Amman
Association Olympique
Suisse Case postale 202
CH - 3000 Berne
Switzerland 32

WORLD WIDE WEB SITE

http://www.swissolympic.ch/d/olympicgames/index.cfm?tid=18&rid=
  15&action=detail

Shannon Bahrke 1980-

American Freestyle Skier
Winner of the Silver Medal in Women's Moguls at the
2002 Winter Olympics

BIRTH

Shannon Bahrke (pronounced *BAR-kee*) was born on November 7, 1980, in Tahoe City, California. Her parents are Richard (known as Dick) and Trilla Bahrke. She has one brother and one sister.

YOUTH

Growing up near the ski resorts surrounding Lake Tahoe, Bahrke learned to ski at the age of three. Surprisingly, she did not really like winter as a girl. She enjoyed accompanying her mother to the slopes mainly because they would stop at the candy shop at the ski lodge afterward.

As Bahrke grew older, it became clear that she was an outstanding natural athlete. The coach of a local ski team, Raymond de Vre, noticed her talent and tried to persuade her to ski competitively. He thought that Bahrke would be particularly good at skiing the event called moguls. These are large, evenly spaced bumps of snow that are typically formed on steep ski hills. Expert skiers must make sharp, aggressive turns to negotiate their way through moguls fields.

——— " ———

"I love skiing moguls. Coming down that course is the hugest adrenaline rush you've ever had in your life. I think all athletes would say the same about their sports. I think mine is especially unique because I love moguls, and we do a whole bunch of different facets, combining the moguls with the air and doing it all with speed. It's truly magnificent."

——— " ———

When Bahrke was 11 years old, she finally gave in to pressure from the coach and agreed to join the ski team. "I didn't want to ski, let alone ski moguls," she recalled. "Those things scared me. But [the coach] kept pestering me and finally I said, 'Okay, I'll do it, if you just stop bothering me.'" Bahrke's skills quickly improved as she trained with the team. "I put her on my ski team and they were all guys, she was one of the only girls," said Coach de Vre. "I treated her like one of the guys and she skied like one of the guys." Five years later, Bahrke was good enough to join the U.S. Ski Team.

EDUCATION

Bahrke attended North Lake Tahoe High School, where she played soccer and softball and ran track. She also played trumpet in the school band and went on a national tour with the band one year. Upon graduating from high school in 1999, Bahrke entered the University of Utah in Salt Lake City. "It's a great school," she explained. "It's really close to everything I need in Salt Lake, it's close to skiing and all of the facilities the U.S. Ski Team has to offer." Bahrke takes college classes during the fall semester,

Bahrke on the women's moguls course at the Salt Lake City Olympics.

then takes the winter off to train and compete with the U.S. Ski Team. She plans to major in pharmacy or public relations.

CAREER HIGHLIGHTS

Career Threatened by a Mysterious Illness

Bahrke began training with the U.S. Ski Team while she was still in high school. In 1998, she finished fifth at the U.S. National Championships in both the moguls and dual moguls (in which two racers go down the course at the same time). In 1999, she placed fifth in dual moguls at the World Championships. But a serious illness nearly ended Bahrke's skiing career later that year. She was driving back to California with her boyfriend, Geoff Lewis, after spending part of the summer at his family's lake house in New Hampshire. Along the way, she came down with a terrible fever and chills. "She had a raging fever," Lewis remembered. "We were driving, and she had a sleeping bag over her and the heat was on. This was in August."

———— " ————

Bahrke says that after she was seriously ill, "Mom is the one who kept telling me that I was going to get through everything, that I was going to get back on those skis and I was going to be here for the Olympics. She pushed and pushed and said, 'You're going to be on that podium. You're going to do it. You can be the best.' And I believed her."

———— " ————

Lewis took Bahrke to a hospital in Pennsylvania, where doctors at first thought she was suffering from meningitis (an infection that involves swelling of the membranes that surround the brain and spinal cord). They gave her antibiotics, and she was able to fly home. Over the next few weeks, however, Bahrke continued to feel poorly and started to feel pain in her lower back. Thinking that the back pain was probably related to the pounding her body took on the ski hill, she visited a chiropractor. But the chiropractor suspected that the problem might be a staphylococcus (staph) infection. Bahrke underwent more tests, and doctors confirmed that staph bacteria had somehow entered her bloodstream and caused an infection at the base of her spine.

Bahrke took more antibiotics, but her condition continued to worsen. She lost about 20 pounds, and she became so weak that she could only walk with the aid of crutches. Doctors finally had to administer powerful antibiotics through a needle directly into her bloodstream. She remained connected to an IV around the clock for six weeks. The doctors told her that she might never be able to walk again, let alone ski competitively. "It was really scary," Bahrke recalled. "Doctors told me they didn't think I'd ever go back to skiing the way I can."

During this difficult time, her family rallied around her and helped keep her spirits up. Her mother encouraged her by telling her that she would one day ski in the 2002 Olympics. "Mom is the one who kept telling me that I was going to get through everything, that I was going to get back on those skis and I was going to be here for the Olympics," she noted. "She pushed and pushed and said, 'You're going to be on that podium. You're going to do it. You can be the best.' And I believed her." Bahrke eventually made a full recovery from her illness, and she returned to competitive skiing after a few months. But the life-threatening experience helped her to appreciate her talent and take her skiing career more seriously. "It made me take every day and look at it in a different way," she admitted. "It makes you realize that your body is so precious."

Making the U.S. Olympic Team

After coming back from her illness, Bahrke finished third in moguls at the U.S. National Championships in 2000. As the 2001 season got underway, Bahrke found herself competing against her American teammates for a spot on the U.S. Olympic Team, which would participate in the 2002 Winter Olympics in Salt Lake City, Utah. She responded by posting the best season of her career. She took first place at the U.S. National Championships in dual moguls and finished fifth in moguls. She also finished in the top 10 in six different events on the World Cup circuit (the top level of international ski competition).

On December 31, 2001, Bahrke won the U.S. Ski Team Gold Cup moguls competition to earn a spot on the Olympic team. "It was fantastic," she recalled. "I had grade school teachers calling me on the phone, little boys and girls running up to me on the street, and then there was my mom, who couldn't stop saying, 'Oh my God, my little baby is going to the Olympics.'" Bahrke's fantastic season continued a week later, when she claimed her first career World Cup victory at an event in Oberstdorf, Germany. In that event she beat Kari Traa of Norway, who was considered the favorite for an Olympic gold medal. She thus became the only woman to defeat the Olympic favorite in a World Cup moguls competition all year. "I'm still the underdog, or as my boyfriend calls me, a dark horse," Bahrke noted. "I don't think I'm considered to be one of the people that could win a medal. I've had a good season, but there are definitely people out there that could do the same thing."

Bahrke found it difficult to wait for the Olympic Games to begin. "I think I've aged ten years just waiting for the Olympics," she stated. "After three years of just missing the top of the World Cup podium and then nailing it down in January, I'm feeling confident going into the Olympic Games and I'm going to ski hard." Like many of her teammates, she found it especially meaningful to represent the United States just a few months after the

Bahrke competing in the women's moguls at the 2002 Olympics.

tragic terrorist attacks of September 11, 2001. "For all of us, I think it means a lot more to be competing for your country," she explained. "Not only are we competing for ourselves, but we're competing for our whole country and a country that is looking up to us for something to believe in, too. I think the Olympics is a great opportunity because we do get to unite all of the nations around the world and show that we can get together in a peaceful atmosphere."

Competing at the Olympics

The Olympic women's moguls competition took place on February 9, 2002, making it the first event of the Salt Lake City Games. It was held on a course called Champion, which was the longest, steepest, and fastest moguls course in international competition. Champion is 261 meters long, and the average angle of descent is 28 degrees. Bahrke hoped that living and training in Salt Lake City would provide her and her teammates with an advantage in the competition. "I love this course," she stated. "I think it really accents all the stuff I've got going for me. I love it. The sun is out and the sky is blue and that's what I do best in."

The Olympic competition consisted of a qualifying round and a final round. The skiers with the top 16 scores in the qualifying round made it to the finals. The skiers with the top three scores in the finals won the Olympic medals. The course consisted of three sections of moguls divided by two jumps. The competitors were required to race through the moguls and perform tricks off of the two jumps. A panel of seven judges scored the competition based on the time required to complete the course (25 percent), the quality of turns in the moguls (50 percent), and the form, difficulty, and landing for the jumps (25 percent). A perfect score was 30 points.

Bahrke showed her patriotic spirit on the hill, with red, white, and blue ribbons braided into her hair and American flags painted on her fingernails. She also wore gold glitter on her cheeks, as she does whenever she competes. "It's good-luck glitter," she explained. At the bottom of the moguls hill were over 13,000 spectators who were hoping for the Americans to earn medals. The crowd included about 150 of Bahrke's friends, relatives, college classmates, and members of her former ski club. Her mother passed out

Bahrke found it especially meaningful to represent the United States just a few months after the tragic terrorist attacks of September 11, 2001. "For all of us, I think it means a lot more to be competing for your country. Not only are we competing for ourselves, but we're competing for our whole country and a country that is looking up to us for something to believe in, too. I think the Olympics is a great opportunity because we do get to unite all of the nations around the world and show that we can get together in a peaceful atmosphere."

50 homemade red, white, and blue fleece hats that said "Go Shannon" on them, and many of her fans held up signs with supportive messages. Bahrke was particularly excited that her grandparents were in the crowd, as they had never seen her compete in person before.

Winning a Silver Medal in Moguls

Bahrke placed fifth in the qualifying round with a score of 23.74. The skiers raced in reverse order in the finals, so that Bahrke competed fifth from last. As she stood at the top of the hill and prepared to make her final run, the TV cameras captured a huge smile on her face. "I just felt that it was my time to do well, and I had to relax and ski the way that I knew that I could. And the only way I knew how to do that was to smile," she explained. "I just told myself this was a great moment to be an American athlete skiing in an Olympics in America. I could hear those countdowns, and I just told myself, 'Go for it.' I just love the speed and I love those turns. I didn't feel pressure. I just wanted to fly down that hill." Bahrke made a flawless run. She whipped through the moguls and performed two impressive jumps, a helicopter iron cross (a 360 degree turn with crossed skis) and a helicopter (360 degree turn). She pumped her fists in the air at the finish line when she saw that her score of 25.06 put her in first place.

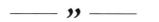

> *As Bahrke prepared to make her final run, the TV cameras captured a huge smile on her face. "I just felt that it was my time to do well, and I had to relax and ski the way that I knew that I could. And the only way I knew how to do that was to smile. I just told myself this was a great moment to be an American athlete skiing in an Olympics in America. I could hear those countdowns, and I just told myself, 'Go for it.' I just love the speed and I love those turns. I didn't feel pressure. I just wanted to fly down that hill."*

Bahrke watched nervously as the four top-ranked skiers tried to beat her score. Her American teammates Hannah Hardaway and Ann Battelle both made mistakes on their jumps and ended up out of the medals. Then the defending gold medalist, Tae Satoya of Japan, also scored lower than Bahrke. The only skier remaining was the favorite, Kari Traa of Norway. Traa made a near-perfect run and posted a score of 25.94 to take the gold medal away from Bahrke. But Bahrke was gracious in accepting the silver medal. "If Kari doesn't make a mistake, then she's gonna be hard to beat. I don't have a problem with how it turned out. I was just delighted to be on the podium," she stated. "When I finished and saw my score and I was number one at that point, I thought I might win the gold. But Kari was about to come down and I was actually rooting for her. Not to beat me. I'm human. I wanted to win. But I owe so much to her, so many skiers do, and she's my friend. When she finished I wanted to hug her, and I did."

Upon receiving her silver medal, Bahrke learned that it was the first medal awarded to an American at the Salt Lake City Games. It was the first medal toward the American team goal of winning 20 medals. "To be the first one to get a medal, to do it when everybody was watching, it makes me so proud, and it gives me hope that the entire team can reach our goal," she noted. "Why not aim high? We've got the world in

Bahrke celebrates after her silver medal run at the 2002 Olympics.

our backyard, playing these Games on our home field, and we might as well lay it all out there and shoot for a number that will stand out there for years." (The United States ultimately ended up with a record 34 medals for the Games.) Bahrke was especially thrilled to win her medal in front of her family and friends. "It's just an amazing feeling, my family standing back behind me," she noted. "It's something you can't put into words, to see the smile on your dad's face while the tears are rolling down his cheeks."

Success Continues Following the Games

A few weeks after the Olympics concluded, Bahrke continued her phenomenal year by winning her second World Cup moguls competition of the season in Madarao, Japan. At the end of March, she successfully defended her national title in dual moguls and also won the national championship in moguls for the first time. "I love skiing moguls," she said. "Coming down that course is the hugest adrenaline rush you've ever had in your life. I think all athletes would say the same about their sports. I think mine is especially unique because I love moguls, and we do a whole bunch of different facets, combining the moguls with the air and doing it all with speed. It's truly magnificent."

Bahrke's love of her sport is apparent in her positive attitude both on and off the ski hill. In fact, she is known for her bubbly personality and earned the nickname "Sparky" among her Olympic teammates. "Shannon's definitely not made to be a monk," said U.S. moguls coach Don St. Pierre. "If I told her to sit down and not say a word, she'd melt. She's a real bright spark, so dynamic, energetic, and chattery." Bahrke plans to continue skiing for as long as she's having fun. "A lot of skiers out there aren't having enough fun, and I'm a firm believer that the more fun I'm having on my skis the better I'm skiing," she explained. "I'll be out there banging moguls in my cool belt, wearing my glitter, singing loud before I drop into a run, that's my style. I pull up to the mountain in my VW beetle and people know I'm on the slopes."

> *Bahrke plans to continue skiing for as long as she's having fun. "A lot of skiers out there aren't having enough fun, and I'm a firm believer that the more fun I'm having on my skis the better I'm skiing. I'll be out there banging moguls in my cool belt, wearing my glitter, singing loud before I drop into a run, that's my style. I pull up to the mountain in my VW beetle and people know I'm on the slopes."*

HOME AND FAMILY

Bahrke is not married, although she has been dating Geoff Lewis for four years. She lives in Salt Lake City, Utah, where she trains with the U.S. Ski Team and attends the University of Utah.

HOBBIES AND OTHER INTERESTS

When she is not on the slopes, Bahrke enjoys mountain biking, windsurfing, waterskiing, shopping, and eating ice cream.

HONORS AND AWARDS

U.S. National Freestyle Skiing Championships: 2000, Third Place (Moguls); 2001, First Place (Dual Moguls); 2002, First Place (Moguls and Dual Moguls)
U.S. Ski Team Gold Cup: 2001, First Place (Moguls)
World Cup Women's Moguls: 2002, First Place at Oberstdorf, Germany, and Madarao, Japan
Olympic Women's Moguls: 2002, Silver Medal

FURTHER READING

Periodicals

Atlanta Journal and Constitution, Feb. 10, 2002, p.D1
Christian Science Monitor, Feb. 12, 2002, p.1
Colorado Springs Gazette, Feb. 9, 2002, Olympics sec., p.4; Feb. 10, 2002,
    Olympics sec., p.4
Daily News of Los Angeles, Feb. 10, 2002, p.S1; June 8, 2002, p.AV1
Houston Chronicle, Feb. 10, 2002 , Special section, p.1
Los Angeles Times, Feb. 10, 2002, p.A1
New York Times, Feb. 10, 2002, p.L8; Feb. 25, 2002, p.A1
Newark Star-Ledger, Feb. 10, 2002, p.O18
San Francisco Chronicle, Feb. 10, 2002, p.B1
Seattle Times, Feb. 10, 2002, p.C1
Sports Illustrated, Feb. 10, 2002, p.5
St. Petersburg (Fla.) Times, Feb. 10, 2002, p.C17
USA Today, Feb. 10, 2002, Bonus sec., p.3
Washington Post, Feb. 10, 2002, p.D1

ADDRESS

Shannon Bahrke
U.S. Ski and Snowboard Association
P.O. Box 100
Park City, UT 84060

WORLD WIDE WEB SITES

http://internal.ussa.org/PR/public/Biosfre.asp?ussaid=5136098
http://www.olympic-usa.org/athlete_profiles/s_bahrke.html
http://cbs.sportsline.com/u/olympics/2002/athletes/bahrke_s.htm

Kelly Clark 1983-

American Snowboarder
Winner of the Gold Medal in the Women's Halfpipe
Event at the 2002 Winter Olympics

BIRTH

Kelly Clark was born on July 26, 1983, in Newport, Rhode
Island. Her family moved to the quiet ski resort town of West
Dover, Vermont, when she was two years old. Her parents,
Terry and Cathy Clark, own a popular restaurant called TC's
Tavern near the Mount Snow ski resort. Cathy waits tables,
tends bar, and does the bookkeeping. Terry does the cooking
and specializes in homemade pizza.

YOUTH

The Clark family lived in a two-story apartment above their restaurant. Kelly learned to ski at an early age and spent as much time as possible on the slopes of Mount Snow. She was a promising young ski racer until she reached third grade. That was the year that Mount Snow first allowed snowboarding. The sport of snowboarding originated in the 1960s, when adventurous young people tried sliding down snow-covered hills on surfboards or on two skis bolted together. For many years, snowboarding was considered an "outlaw" sport and was not allowed at most ski resorts. But as the equipment improved and more trend-setting youngsters took up the sport, it rapidly gained in popularity and acceptance.

Clark first tried snowboarding at the age of nine. She loved the freedom of the relatively new sport. She also appreciated the fact that snowboarders tended to be less competitive and more laid back than ski racers. Before long, she started skipping ski team practices in order to go snowboarding. "It was almost like a rebelling type deal for me to start boarding," Clark recalled. "At nine, I was putting a lot of effort into skiing, and my parents were big skiers. When I saw boarding, it just looked so cool that I had to try it."

"It was almost like a rebelling type deal for me to start boarding. At nine, I was putting a lot of effort into skiing, and my parents were big skiers. When I saw boarding, it just looked so cool that I had to try it."

At first, Clark's parents were not pleased about her decision to switch sports. "My parents were totally against it," she remembered. "They told me I could try boarding but that I was going back to be a ski racer." Terry Clark told his daughter, "Kelly, I know how much you like snowboarding, but it's just a fad. It's never gonna take off. Stick with skiing." But her parents gradually changed their minds as snowboarding gained popularity and Kelly made it clear that she was hooked on the sport.

EDUCATION

Shortly after Mount Snow allowed "shredders" (a slang term for snowboarders) on its slopes, Clark started a snowboarding club at Dover Elementary School. She went on to attend Brattleboro Union High School, where she played soccer and tennis. She completed her final years of high school at the Mount Snow Academy, a special school for top skiers and snowboarders. The academy allowed Clark to divide her days between training on her snowboard and being tutored in academic subjects. She graduated from high school in the spring of 2001.

Clark was accepted to the Rhode Island School of Design, an acclaimed college for art and design. But she chose to defer her college admission until after her snowboarding career is over. "I will be able to go to school for the rest of my life, but I'll only be young once," she explained. When Clark eventually attends college, she plans to major in art and design.

"There's a certain fear factor you have to let go of, and you have to be really confident in yourself in the air. Once you break through that level of fear and feel comfortable with yourself, you can really push the limit."

CAREER HIGHLIGHTS

Becoming a Top Competitor in Halfpipe Events

Clark began competing in international snowboarding competitions while she was still in high school. Her specialty was the halfpipe. In this event, snowboarders glide back and forth through a 500-foot-long, U-shaped tube of snow. They gain speed on the downward slopes and perform tricks at the top of the upward slopes. Competitors typically perform six to eight tricks before reaching the bottom of the pipe. They are judged on the height of their jumps; the variety, difficulty, and execution of their tricks; and the cleanness of their landings. Five judges each award a maximum of 10 points, which are added together to get a final score.

From the beginning of her career, Clark was considered one of the most aggressive female riders. She was especially known for her outstanding amplitude, or her height in the air above the pipe while performing tricks. In fact, Clark often reached an amplitude of eight to nine feet, while most of her competitors could only achieve five to six feet. "I learned how to go big, to make the airs. It made sense to me that once you have your amplitude down, when you try the tricks, they're a lot easier, because you have more time to do them," she stated. "There's a certain fear factor you have to let go of, and you have to be really confident in yourself in the air. Once you break through that level of fear and feel comfortable with yourself, you can really push the limit."

In addition to halfpipe events, Clark also competed in snowboardcross (SBX) early in her career. This event has been compared to roller derby on

Clark competing in the finals of the women's snowboarding halfpipe event at the 2002 Olympics.

snow. Six competitors are released at the top of a hill at the same time. They race through a series of gates, around turns, and over obstacles. Pushing and shoving is an accepted part of the competition. In many cases, the competitor who remains upright on her snowboard is the win-

35

———— **"** ————

*Clark plays the song
"This Is Growing Up"
by Blink 182 on her mini-
disc player every time she
competes. "Every time
before I drop into the pipe,
I turn up my mini disc,
and I try not to pay attention
to what's going on around
me. When I'm more relaxed
I ride better, so if I'm kind
of in my own zone, it's like
any other day for me. . . ."*

———— **"** ————

ner. Clark used her small size and quick moves to her advantage in SBX competitions. As her halfpipe skills improved, however, she stopped competing in snowboardcross due to the high potential for injury.

Clark first gained notice in the snowboarding world when she won the junior world championship in halfpipe in 2000. She also claimed the U.S. national championship in snowboardcross that year. Her success led to an invitation to train with the U.S. Snowboard Team. Clark's fine performances continued in 2001, when she won the U.S. national championship in both snowboardcross and halfpipe. She also claimed her first World Cup victory by winning the halfpipe competition in Sapporo, Japan. She finished the 2001 season by winning three consecutive events in the American Grand Prix series. Her fine performances helped her clinch a spot on the U.S. Snowboard Team that would compete in the 2002 Winter Olympic Games in Salt Lake City, Utah.

Competing in the 2002 Winter Olympics

The International Olympic Committee added snowboarding to the Winter Olympic program in 1998 in an attempt to modernize the Games. But some shredders were upset to see snowboarding in the Olympics because they felt the international spotlight would ruin the casual, laid-back nature of their sport. In fact, several top riders chose not to compete in the 1998 Games. By 2002, however, most athletes decided that participating in the Olympics would give their sport positive attention and added respectability. For her part, Clark was thrilled to be selected as a member of the U.S. Olympic Team. "It's pretty overwhelming," she said at the time. "I'm not really sure what to say. It hasn't really hit me, but I think it's pretty great."

In February 2002, Clark traveled to Salt Lake City and began practicing for the Olympic halfpipe competition. Just a few days before the start of the Games, Clark crashed in practice and suffered a severe bruise on her tailbone, which is at the base of the spine. The impact was so jarring that she laid on the snow for 20 minutes before she could even stand up. She went to the hospital for X-rays, which showed no broken bones. But Clark was still very sore on the day before the Olympic halfpipe competition and worried whether she would be able to perform. "When I was lying on my stomach in bed that night, I was thinking, 'Ohhh, what am I going to do?' I was kind of miserable. What bad timing," she recalled.

Clark was still feeling the effects of her injury on the day of the women's halfpipe competition, but she was so excited that she was able to forget about her pain. She faced a field of 23 competitors from 12 countries around the world. The women all took part in a qualifying round, then the top riders advanced to the finals. Each finalist was allowed to make two runs through the halfpipe, and only their best score would count in deciding the medal winners. Clark ended up posting the highest score in the qualifying round to advance easily. She then made a solid first run in the finals, for which the judges awarded her 40.8 out of a possible 50 points. This score put her in second place behind the reigning world champion, Doriane Vidal of France, who had posted a score of 43.0 in her first run.

In the second round, Vidal failed to improve her score but remained on top of the standings. All of the other competitors completed their runs through the halfpipe, but none were able to surpass Clark's first round score of 40.8. As Clark prepared to make her final run, she knew that she already had the silver medal wrapped up. This knowledge gave her the freedom to attempt a very difficult series of tricks, including a frontside 720 (two forward flips in mid-air). "Going into my last run, I knew that I was going to get no worse than second, so I figured I really had to go all out, really give it all I had. I had to or I would regret it if I didn't, so I worked on cleaning my run up," she remembered. "I had amplitude on my side, but my technical riding wasn't there, so I needed another technical trick. I knew that going into it and I pulled out the seven [the 720]."

"[At the Olympics] I had my headphones on full blast, and usually I can't hear someone talking to me a foot away. But I could hear the crowd roaring over the headphones. Every time I hit the wall I could hear the crowd go, 'Aah!' Then I'd come back down and go back across, and they'd go, 'Aah!' It was crazy. They were so amazing, I'd never heard anything like it."

Clark gains amplitude during the finals of the women's halfpipe competition.

Making History with Her Gold Medal Run

With the song "Welcome to the Jungle" by the hard rock band Guns 'n' Roses blaring over the loudspeakers, Clark launched herself into the half-pipe for the final run of the women's competition. She achieved huge amplitude and completed seven flawless tricks. She started with a frontside air (in which the rider leaps forward and rests her back on the board), then performed an indy air (the rider leaps backward with her hand gripping the board), moved into a 540 frontside grab (the rider completes one-and-a-half forward spins while grabbing the board), then did a backside method (the rider grabs the back of board with her hand and pulls it level with her head) and a frontside stalefish (the rider grabs the heel side of the board while rising above the pipe). She finished her run with back-to-back inverted tricks, a McTwist indy grab (the rider spins around twice while grabbing the board) and the frontside 720.

The crowd of nearly 20,000 spectators went wild as she landed each trick successfully. In fact, the crowd was so loud that Clark could hear them over the music on her headphones (she plays the song "This Is Growing Up" by Blink 182 on her mini-disc player every time she competes). "Every time before I drop into the pipe, I turn up my mini disc, and I try not to pay attention to what's going on around me. When I'm more relaxed I ride better, so if I'm kind of in my own zone, it's like any other day for me," she explained. "I had my headphones on full blast, and usually I can't hear someone talking to me a foot away. But I could hear the crowd roaring over the headphones. Every time I hit the wall I could hear the crowd go, 'Aah!' Then I'd come back down and go back across, and they'd go, 'Aah!' It was crazy. They were so amazing, I'd never heard anything like it."

Clark dedicated her gold medal to her fellow Americans who were affected by the terrorist attacks of September 11, 2001. "It means a whole lot to me. We've had a tough few months here. It's great to give people something to cheer about."

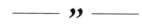

When the judges' scores were totaled, Clark had earned an amazing 47.9 points — one of the highest scores ever awarded in the history of women's halfpipe. She had also achieved a dramatic come-from-behind victory to claim the gold medal. Clark thus became the first American ever to win a gold medal in snowboarding, as well as the first American to earn gold in the 2002 Olympic Games. "I'm so psyched," she said afterward. "It's so amazing. I can't even explain what I'm feeling right now." Doriane Vidal of France had to settle for silver, and Fabienne Reuteler of Switzerland took bronze.

Clark dedicated her gold medal to her fellow Americans who were affected by the terrorist attacks of September 11, 2001. "It means a whole lot to me," she stated. "We've had a tough few months here. It's great to give people something to cheer about." Clark also hoped that her performance would have a positive effect on her sport. "Snowboarders have their reputations," she admitted. "But my doing this, especially in the U.S., says a lot. Maybe it will shine a light on snowboarding, and people will look at it in a different way." The day after she became the first American to earn a gold medal in snowboarding, Clark watched as three of her teammates — Ross Powers, Danny Kass, and J.J. Thomas — swept the medals in the men's halfpipe competition.

> *Clark hoped that her performance would have a positive effect on her sport. "Snowboarders have their reputations. But my doing this, especially in the U.S., says a lot. Maybe it will shine a light on snowboarding, and people will look at it in a different way."*

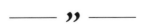

Sharing Her Love of Snowboarding

In the weeks following her Olympic triumph, Clark received a great deal of media attention. One of her most memorable experiences came during an interview on the *Tonight Show* with Jay Leno, when she was surprised on stage by singer Britney Spears. Clark was pleased that her success in the Olympics helped showcase the sport of snowboarding. "I think the Olympics have done a lot for the sport," she noted. "Everyone I talked to says all their kids want to do now is snowboard. It's really great to hear. It's amazing. I hope to keep snowboarding for as long as I have fun and make a few more Olympics."

Clark returned to competition a few weeks after the Olympics and continued her winning ways. She earned a gold medal in superpipe at the 2002 Winter X Games and won the halfpipe competition at the U.S. Open Snowboarding Championships. "I really want to keep progressing," she stated. "I don't want to ever stop moving forward. Especially in women's snowboarding. [It] is progressing so fast, I want to contribute to that. I

never want to stop learning. I am young with a lot of ambition, so I'm really looking forward to learning a lot of new tricks and trying new things."

HOME AND FAMILY

Clark, who is single, moved from Vermont to Mammoth Lakes, California, in 2001 in order to train with the U.S. Snowboarding Team.

HOBBIES AND OTHER INTERESTS

In her spare time, Clark enjoys surfing and listening to music. She is also a big fan of the New York Yankees, especially shortstop Derek Jeter.

HONORS AND AWARDS

World Junior Halfpipe Championship: 2000, first place
Goodwill Games Women's Halfpipe: 2000, Silver Medal; 2002, Gold
    Medal
U.S. National Snowboarding Championship: 2000, first place in snow-
    boardcross; 2001, first place in halfpipe and snowboardcross

41

Olympic Women's Halfpipe: 2002, Gold Medal
ESPY Award: 2002, for best action sports athlete

FURTHER READING

Periodicals

Boston Globe, Feb. 1, 2001, p.E10; Mar. 26, 2001, p.D7; Feb. 11, 2002, p.D1
Denver Rocky Mountain News, Feb. 11, 2002, p.S2
Detroit Free Press, Feb. 21, 2002
Los Angeles Times, Feb. 11, 2002, p.U1
New York Times, Feb. 11, 2002, p.D1
St. Louis Post-Dispatch, Feb. 11, 2002, p.D1
San Francisco Chronicle, Feb. 11, 2002, p.C6
Seattle Post-Intelligencer, Feb. 11, 2002, p.A1
Sports Illustrated, Feb. 18, 2002, p.42
USA Today, Feb. 11, 2002, p.D4
Washington Post, Feb. 11, 2002, p.A1
WWD, Feb. 13, 2002, p.4

Online Articles

http://www.mountsnow.org/Programs/Snowboard/NewsS/KellyClark.htm
 (*MountSnow.org,* "Olympic Gold for Clark in Halfpipe!"Feb. 10, 2002)
http://www.mountainzone.com/olympics/2002/html/sb_w_hp.html
 (*Mountainzone.com,* "Kelly Clark Takes Gold for U.S.,"Feb. 10, 2002)

ADDRESS

Kelly Clark
U.S. Ski and Snowboard Association
P.O. Box 100
Park City, UT 84060

WORLD WIDE WEB SITES

http://internal.ussa.org/PR/public/Biosbrd.asp?ussaid=5506175
http://sports.yahoo.com/oly/snowboarding/usoc/bios/f/k_clark.html
http://cbs.sportsline.com/u/olympics/2002/athletes/clark_ke.htm
http://expn.go.com/athletes/snb/index.html
http://www.olympic-usa.org

Vonetta Flowers 1973-

American Bobsledder and Track and Field Athlete
Winner of the Gold Medal in the Women's Bobsled at
the 2002 Winter Olympics
First Black Athlete Ever to Win a Gold Medal at the
Winter Olympics

BIRTH

Vonetta Flowers was born Vonetta Jeffery on October 29, 1973,
in Birmingham, Alabama. Her parents, Jimmie and Barbara
Jeffery, divorced when she was a child. She and her three
brothers grew up with their mother.

YOUTH

Even as a young child, Flowers was an exceptional athlete. She loved playing all sorts of games with her neighborhood friends, and her mother enrolled her in a variety of city-sponsored leagues and events. This gave Flowers the opportunity to participate in track and field events, and the youngster quickly developed a fierce love for running. In fact, by age nine Flowers was posting such fast times in the 50-yard dash that a city league track coach mistakenly thought that the time belonged to a 13-year-old boy. This track coach, DeWitt Thomas of the Birmingham Striders Track Club, eventually became her first coach for track events.

Flowers joined the Birmingham Striders, a summer track team, when she was nine years old. "From then on I lived and breathed track," she recalled. As a member of the Striders, Flowers continued to show amazing speed and athletic ability in an assortment of sprint and jumping events. By her mid-teens she had become a dominant figure in local and regional junior meets.

> *"Sometimes, like when I couldn't go to my senior prom because of a [track] meet, it bothered me that I missed out on normal high school stuff. But I also knew that if I was going to get to the Olympics, sacrifices come with the territory. And my parents have always encouraged me to follow my dreams."*

Thomas was delighted with Flowers's progress, and he enjoyed coaching her because of her strong work ethic and her warm and friendly personality. One day, he told her that she possessed the talent to be the next Jackie Joyner-Kersee, an African-American track and field star who had won Olympic gold in the heptathlon event in 1988 and 1992. This compliment thrilled Flowers and sparked dreams that she might one day be an Olympian herself.

At times, the demands of track and field forced Flowers to make sacrifices in other aspects of her life. "Sometimes, like when I couldn't go to my senior prom because of a meet, it bothered me that I missed out on normal high school stuff," she admitted. "But I also knew that if I was going to get to the Olympics, sacrifices come with the territory. And my parents have always encouraged me to follow my dreams."

EDUCATION

Flowers attended elementary school in the Birmingham public school system, then moved on to Birmingham's Jackson-Olin High School. During
her years at Jackson-Olin, she emerged as a nationally recognized track
star and an All-State basketball player.

After earning her high school diploma in 1992, Flowers enrolled at the
University of Alabama-Birmingham (UAB), where she received a full
scholarship. She enjoyed a spectacular freshman year in track and field,
breaking three school records for freshmen and earning Great Midwest
Conference Newcomer of the Year honors in 1993. As her college career
continued, she became a dominant performer in several events, including
the 100-meter dash, 200-meter dash, long jump, and triple jump. By the
time she graduated in 1997 with a bachelor of science degree in physical
education, she had been named a seven-time NCAA All-American, six-
time Great Midwest Conference Most Valuable Player, and Most Outstanding Athlete at the Great Midwest Conference Outdoor Championships. All told, she earned 35 conference championship awards in various
track and field events during her four years at Alabama-Birmingham.
Years later, Flowers continues to hold half a dozen individual track and
field records at the school.

CAREER HIGHLIGHTS

During her years as a student-athlete at Alabama-Birmingham, Flowers
competed in numerous track and field events featuring the country's top
sprinters and jumpers. In fact, she qualified to compete in nine different
U.S. Track and Field national championship events, and in 1995 she qualified for the World University Games. But she also suffered a series of injuries during her college career, including ligament damage to her hips,
knees, and ankles. These physical problems contributed to her failure to
qualify for the 1996 Summer Olympics.

In 1997 Flowers accepted a job as a graduate assistant with the University
of Alabama's men's track team. She worked in this capacity for the next
two years, coaching a variety of field events and serving as the team's head
equipment manager. In 1999 she returned to her alma mater, the University of Alabama-Birmingham, where she was hired as an assistant coach
for the school's cross country and track teams.

Flowers enjoyed working with the school's young athletes, and she found
coaching to be a rewarding career. But she still harbored dreams of achiev-
ing athletic glory. Despite suffering a series of nagging injuries, she contin-

*Flowers (left) and Bakken (right) push off during the women's
bobsled event at the 2002 Olympics.*

ued to nurture her dream of being an Olympic athlete. In the late 1990s she switched her training emphasis from sprinting to the long jump. But she was forced to undergo ankle surgery only five months before the track and field trials for the 2000 Summer Olympics.

After her surgery, Flowers labored mightily to prepare for the Olympic try-outs, which were to be held in Sacramento, California. "At 26 years old, I knew this was going to be my last shot at qualifying for the Summer Games." But despite her best efforts, she finished a disappointing 12th in the competition and failed to make the team once again.

Venturing into the World of Bobsledding

While still in Sacramento, however, Flowers and her husband, Johnny Flowers, learned that one of the country's leading bobsled athletes, Bonny Warner, was holding open tryouts in the city for a pushing spot on her two-person sled. Vonetta Flowers had never even ridden in a bobsled before, but her husband urged her to give it a try. She agreed, thinking that it might be kind of fun. But she actually performed very well in the tests, and Warner invited her to take a trial run on the Olympic bobsled track.

At first, Flowers was not certain that she wanted to pursue the bobsledding experiment any further. "The only thing I knew about the Winter Olympics was the movie *Cool Runnings,* you know, the one about the no-chance Jamaican bobsled team," recalled Flowers. She also was not sure that she wanted to spend all of her time in the cold, snowy places where bobsled training and competitions are held. She liked Alabama's warm climate and knew that she would miss it if she was gone for very long. Meanwhile, Warner harbored doubts about Flowers as well. "She was so quiet and shy and sweet," Warner recalled. "I wasn't sure she would like it."

But Flowers eventually agreed to give bobsledding a try, and before she knew it, she was flying down a steep icy course with the wind whipping her face and her heart pounding like a jackhammer. "It's very scary and exhilarating!" said Flowers. "The bobsled can go at extremely high speeds—up to 85 miles per hour. When you take off, gravity pulls your head and body to the ground for a few seconds. It feels as if someone is sitting on your back. After my first ride, I was sore and dizzy for a whole week and I was having doubts. But everyone told me you have to try it twice to really appreciate it. Each run got better because I knew what to expect. . . . I started to love the speed and the twists and turns of the track. It's the same thrill I used to get on roller coasters as a kid."

A New Force in Bobsledding

Flowers agreed to train with Warner for the upcoming international bob-sledding season. They traveled to Germany for a period of intensive train-ing, and during this time, the former track star learned all about the sport.

———— " ————

"It's very scary and exhilarating!" Flowers said after she first tried bobsledding. "The bobsled can go at extremely high speeds — up to 85 miles per hour. When you take off, gravity pulls your head and body to the ground for a few seconds. It feels as if someone is sitting on your back. After my first ride, I was sore and dizzy for a whole week and I was having doubts. . . . I started to love the speed and the twists and turns of the track. It's the same thrill I used to get on roller coasters as a kid."

———— " ————

Two-person bobsled teams in both men's and women's competitions in-clude a driver and a brakeman. From the starting line, the teammates push the sled for up to 50 meters, then quickly hop in to the sled for the downhill run. Getting off to a good start is critical, not only because cham-pionships are often won by tenths or even hundredths of a second, but also because an explosive start can help teams overcome minor steering mis-takes. During a typical run, speeds of up to 85 miles per hour can be reached, and on some turns down the steep, twisting track, competitors are pushed by up to four times the force of gravity. Bobsledding races consist of two runs for each team, with the win-ner determined by the best combined time for both runs.

Warner was an experienced bobsled driver who recognized that Flowers packed a rare combination of power and speed that made her an ideal brakeman for bobsledding competi-tions. Moreover, Flowers showed that she was dedicated to improving her-self. Over the course of several months, she used weight training to add 25 additional pounds of muscle to her athletic figure. With each passing day, Warner and Flowers became more confident that they could hold their own in international competition.

Early in the 2000-2001 World Cup bobsledding season, Flowers and Warner caught the attention of bobsledders all around the world when they broke the world start record at the track at Park City, Utah. As the season progressed the duo won four World Cup medals and registered top 10 finishes in all seven World Cup races. The Warner-Flowers team finished the year ranked third in the world.

Based on their fine performance in the 2000-2001 campaign, Flowers was excited about the 2001-2002 season. In October 2001, however, Warner asked her to compete with another brakeman named Gea Johnson for the second spot on her sled. This was not an unusual request in the world of international bobsledding. In fact, drivers sometimes replaced brakemen who were lifelong friends if they thought that another brakeman gave them a better chance of winning. But Flowers was stunned and hurt by Warner's request, and she abruptly quit the sport rather than submit to the competition against Johnson.

Bakken (front) and Flowers (rear) push off during a training run for the women's bobsled event.

Finding a New Partner

"I went back to Alabama, to my job as assistant track coach at UAB," recalled Flowers. "At that point, that was it for me and bobsled. It wasn't my life. It didn't mean that much. I wanted to start a family." But her husband encouraged her to stay in shape for bobsledding competition. He had a hunch that it would not be long before another bobsled driver came along. As it turned out, Johnny Flowers was right. Shortly after her return to Birmingham, Flowers received a call from Jill Bakken, a 25-year-old American bobsledder with a passion for fast, exciting sports. Bakken asked her to compete with another brakeman for the second slot on her sled. Flowers won the competition, and a few months later, she and Bakken qualified for one of the two spots on Team USA's Winter Olympics squad. The other spot on Team USA went to the highly publicized team of Jean Racine and Gea Johnson. This media attention was due not only to the belief that Racine and Johnson were medal contenders, but also to the fact that Racine had dumped her longtime sledding partner in favor of Johnson only weeks before the Olympics were set to begin.

Flowers and Bakken during their run in the women's bobsled finals at the 2002 Olympics.

Flowers was tremendously excited at the prospect of representing her country in the Olympics. She also expressed amazement at the path that had brought her to the brink of Olympic competition. Instead of competing in a track and field event in the Summer Olympics, she was going to be participating in the Winter Olympics' first-ever bobsled competition for women, 70 years after men's bobsled competitions at the Olympics began in 1932.

The women's bobsled competition event was scheduled for February 19, one of the last days of Olympic competition. As a result, Flowers and Bakken could only train and wait anxiously for their day to come. "I'm so excited," Flowers said a few days before the competition. "The days are going by so slow. It seems like it's been a month. We're sitting in the [Olympic] village watching everybody compete. I can't wait until it's our turn."

A few days before the bobsled competition, however, Flowers received a surprise telephone call from Jean Racine, the driver of the other USA sled. Racine revealed that her partner, Gea Johnson, had injured her hamstring muscle in practice. Flowers knew about the injury and expressed her sympathies. But Racine then shocked Flowers by asking her to dump Bakken and join her bobsled as brakeman, replacing Johnson. "The conversation lasted about four minutes," Flowers recalled. "I told her no. I was going to be loyal to Jill."

Flying to Olympic Gold

Finally, the day arrived when Flowers fulfilled her lifelong dream of competing in the Olympics. She and Bakken knew that nobody expected them to win a medal. Racine and Johnson were still regarded as the United States' best hope for a medal, and German teams had won every World Cup race during the 2001-2002 season. But Flowers and Bakken were not intimidated. Boosted by Flowers's tremendous starting power and Bakken's steady driving, they performed flawlessly in both of their runs. In fact, they set a new world record with their first run. "I'd made about 100 runs in my bobsledding career, but our [first] Olympic ride felt different than all the others," stated Flowers. "I remember pushing harder and faster than I ever had before. And the run itself was perfect. . . . We didn't make a single mistake. Seconds after crossing the finish line, our three team coaches dashed over to us, screaming that we'd broken the world record, just set by the German team, by three tenths of a second. In the world of bobsledding, three tenths of a second is a very big margin and I was confident that no one would catch up to us. I was right: That first run put us over the top and we stayed there."

"I'd made about 100 runs in my bobsledding career, but our [first] Olympic ride felt different than all the others. I remember pushing harder and faster than I ever had before. And the run itself was perfect. . . . We didn't make a single mistake. Seconds after crossing the finish line, our three team coaches dashed over to us, screaming that we'd broken the world record, just set by the German team, by three tenths of a second. In the world of bobsledding, three tenths of a second is a very big margin and I was confident that no one would catch up to us. I was right: That first run put us over the top and we stayed there."

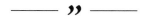

When the competition was over, the partnership of Flowers and Bakken had shocked the bobsledding world with a gold medal-winning time of one minute, 37.76 seconds for their two runs. The two heavily favored German teams claimed the silver and bronze medals, while Jean Racine and Gea Johnson could only manage a fifth-place finish.

The victory by Flowers and Bakken sparked a wild celebration among athletes and fans alike at the finish line. Bakken grinned and laughed, while Flowers cried tears of joy at her accomplishment. "I am so blessed to be here," she exclaimed. "Our goal was to come here and medal. A lot of people saw us as the other team. We came here to prove them wrong."

> "To win a gold medal for your country is simply awesome. Hopefully, this will encourage other African-American boys and girls to give winter sports a try. You don't see too many of them out there. . . . I have truly been blessed to come into this sport and pick it up so fast. My goal was to make the Summer Olympics. God had a different plan for me."

A Historic Win

Shortly after Flowers and Bakken clinched gold, Olympic authorities announced that Flowers had become the first black athlete in Winter Olympics history to win a gold medal. This stunning news overwhelmed the modest Alabama native, who found herself wiping tears from her face throughout the medal ceremony and countless interviews. "To win a gold medal for your country is simply awesome," she explained. "Hopefully, this will encourage other African-American boys and girls to give winter sports a try. You don't see too many of them out there. . . . I have truly been blessed to come into this sport and pick it up so fast. My goal was to make the Summer Olympics. God had a different plan for me."

Back in Alabama, meanwhile, Flowers's friends and family—and the entire UAB track and field team—rejoiced at her triumph. "Some day my kids will be reading about [Flowers] in their history books," said Yolanda Cooper, a senior sprinter on the UAB team. "I'll never forget that moment the rest of my life. Seeing [her win the gold medal] makes me feel like I can accomplish anything." Another member of the UAB team expressed satisfaction that Flowers's true personality was shining through in all the interviews. "I'm just glad with the way she is being portrayed, because she is very humble and happy all the time."

Flowers and Bakken celebrate winning gold during the medals ceremony at the 2002 Winter Olympics.

Adjusting to the Spotlight

In the weeks following the 2002 Winter Olympics' closing ceremonies, Flowers was whisked all around the country for interviews and special events. She and some of her fellow Olympians were special guests at the White House, where they met President George W. Bush. In addition, the city of Birmingham declared March 23, 2002, "Vonetta Flowers Day" and held a big celebration in her honor. The ceremony was attended by an estimated 3,000 people, who gave her a standing ovation. Emotionally overwhelmed by the reception, Flowers cried through much of the event, especially whenever speakers talked about what her achievement meant to others. Finally, she rose to deliver her own remarks. "In Utah, tons of people told me they loved me who didn't even know me," she said with tears in her eyes. "To come back home to faces I know and hear that you love me, it means so much."

Some of the recognition that Flowers received after the Olympics was kind of silly, such as her being named to *People* magazine's annual list of the "50 Most Beautiful People." But she recognized that her accomplishment was significant and that her success made her a role model to young black people all across the United States. "All of this is nice and fun, but it's really an honor to be a part of history. Sometimes, you get mentioned in the same sentence as Jesse Owens [an African-American athlete who won four gold medals at the 1936 Summer Olympics] and all those wonderful people, and it's like, 'Wow.' Sometimes, it's hard to believe."

> *After the Olympics, Flowers discovered that she had actually been pregnant with twins when she and Bakken won the gold medal. "Winning the gold medal was wonderful, but this is a whole new joy. We're excited. We wanted a family after the Games, and God answered our prayers."*

After her return to UAB, Flowers also discovered that she had actually been pregnant with twins when she and Bakken won the gold medal. "Winning the gold medal was wonderful, but this is a whole new joy," she said. "We're excited. We wanted a family after the Games, and God answered our prayers."

Flowers has expressed interest in returning to the Winter Olympics in 2006, when the games will be held in Turin, Italy. But she admits that the next Olympics seems a long ways off, especially since she is starting a family.

MARRIAGE AND FAMILY

Flowers is married to Johnny Mack Flowers, who was a member of the UAB football and track teams. "We met our freshman year, on the first day of track practice," remembers Flowers. He currently works as an administrator for Blue Cross and as his wife's personal trainer. They live in Helena, Alabama, a small town outside of Birmingham. Their twin boys, Jaden Michael and Jorden Maddox, were born on August 30, 2002. Afterward, the new mother was elated. "I experienced the best feeling ever giving birth to my boys," Flowers said. "It tops the Olympic gold medal I won." Her husband had a slightly different perspective. "I was so happy to be able to witness this miracle and catch it all on tape," said Johnny Flowers. "Anybody willing to give birth should have no trouble strapping on the helmet and riding down the track at 80 miles per hour. The experience has opened my eyes to many things and has given me a new respect for mothers!"

HOBBIES AND OTHER INTERESTS

Flowers has actively participated in the University of Alabama-Birmingham's efforts to help inner-city children get involved in track and field competitions and other programs that boost self-esteem.

HONORS AND AWARDS

USA Track and Field Championships: seven-time qualifier, 1993-1997
Great Midwest Conference Newcomer of the Year: 1993
Great Midwest Conference Most Valuable Player, Track and Field: 1994, 1995, 1996, 1997
Olympic Bobsled: 2002, Gold Medal
U.S. Olympic Spirit Award: 2002

In addition, Flowers won 35 Great Midwest Conference championships in various track and field events, and she was a seven-time NCAA All-American

FURTHER READING

Periodicals

Atlanta Journal-Constitution, Feb. 20, 2002, p.C1; Feb. 21, 2002, p.A1; Feb. 28, 2002, p.A1
Chicago Tribune, Mar. 13, 2002, p.C3
Denver Rocky Mountain News, Feb. 21, 2002, p.S4
Detroit Free Press, Feb. 6, 2002, p.G14; Feb. 21, 2002, p.D1
Ebony, May 2002, p.120
Essence, July 2002, p.29
Jet, Mar. 11, 2002, p.51; Apr. 15, 2002, p.8
Ladies' Home Journal, July 2002, p.50
Los Angeles Times, Feb. 21, 2002, p.U1
Milwaukee Journal Sentinel, Feb. 24, 2002, p.1
New York Times, Feb. 20, 2002, p.A1; Feb. 21, 2002, p.D5
O, The Oprah Magazine, July 2002, p.161
People, Mar. 11, 2002, p.62; May 13, 2002, p.167
Philadelphia Inquirer, Feb. 17, 2002, p.D1
San Francisco Chronicle, Feb. 25, 2002, p.A1
Seattle Times, Feb. 21, 2002, p.D6
Sports Illustrated, May 1, 2002, p.6
USA Today, Feb. 20, 2002, p.D1
Washington Post, Feb. 21, 2002, p.D10

Online Articles

http://www.africana.com (*Africana.com,* "Flowers Is No Fluke: A History of Black Bobsledders,"Feb. 22, 2002)
http://www.educationupdate.com/mar02/sports_flowers.html (*Education Update,* "Vonetta Flowers: Bobsledder,"Mar. 2002)
http://www.msnbc.com/news/711453.asp?cp1=1 (*MSNBC.com,* "'Other'U.S. Bobsledders Win Gold,"Feb. 19, 2002)

ADDRESS

Vonetta Flowers
U.S. Bobsled and Skeleton Federation
421 Old Military Road
Lake Placid, NY 12946

WORLD WIDE WEB SITES

http://www.vonettaflowers.com
http://www.olympic-usa.org
http://www.usbsf.com

Cammi Granato 1971-

American Hockey Player
Winner of the Olympic Gold Medal in 1998 and the
Silver Medal in 2002 in Women's Ice Hockey
Captain of the 1998 Gold Medal-Winning Women's
Ice Hockey Team

BIRTH

Catherine Michelle Granato was born in Downers Grove, Illi-
nois, on March 25, 1971. She was the fifth of six children born
to Don, who worked as a beer distributor, and Natalie Granato. Her nickname "Cammi" was invented by her father, who

combined the first two letters of her first and middle names. Granato's siblings include four brothers—Tony, Donny, Joey, and Robby—and one sister, Christina.

YOUTH

Granato was an active, athletic youngster who loved to participate in all sorts of sports. She was a fine basketball player and a star on her little league baseball team. But hockey was by far the number one sport with her and the rest of the Granato household. "There were six kids in my family, and we lived, breathed, ate, and drank hockey," recalled Granato. "My parents' first date was at a Chicago Blackhawks hockey game. We had season tickets to the Blackhawks and we went to all the games. We fell in love with hockey as a family."

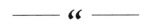

> *"There were six kids in my family, and we lived, breathed, ate, and drank hockey. My parents' first date was at a Chicago Blackhawks hockey game. We had season tickets to the Blackhawks and we went to all the games. We fell in love with hockey as a family."*

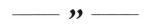

During the winter, all the Granato children spent their days playing hockey on a pond across the street from their home in Downers Grove. "We were on the pond all day," remembered Granato. "We'd come in for supper and sit at the table with our skates on and then go back across the street to play some more. Everything our family did was hockey, hockey, hockey."

The Granatos' passion for hockey even extended deep into the summertime. Cammi and her brothers often attended summer hockey camps, and they spent many sunny afternoons in the basement of their home, where they made up a rink using tape on the walls and floor. They used short pieces of wood for hockey sticks and a rolled-up wad of Kleenex wrapped in tape as a puck. "It was a couple hours, every day," said Granato. "We definitely had some bumps along the boards. But I couldn't really go upstairs and tell Mom somebody hit me. I had to stay and battle it out."

Female hockey players were very rare when Granato was growing up, so her mother tried to steer her into figure skating when she was four or five years old. She bought Cammi a nice skating outfit, complete with skirt and little pom-poms for her skates, and enrolled her in lessons. But this attempt to direct her attention away from hockey was a total failure. "When I was at the lessons, the minute my mom would turn her head, I would be off watching the hockey game at the adjacent rink," recalled Granato. "So she'd come and put me back on the ice, but the minute she would turn her head again I would be right back at the hockey rink. I guess she got the hint because she allowed me to sign up for hockey."

The Granato household's love for hockey reached a new peak in 1980, when a young, lightly regarded American team defeated the legendary Soviet hockey team in the Winter Olympics. This thrilling upset turned the entire Granato home upside down for days, and it sparked Cammi's first dreams of Olympic glory. Another source of inspiration for Granato was her brothers. All three of her older brothers starred on the University of Wisconsin hockey team, and one of them—Tony Granato—played for 13 years in the National Hockey League. "My brothers have been role models all through my life," she said. "I saw how much they accomplished and how successful they were in hockey. And I saw them become captains of their teams at Wisconsin in their senior years. They set the standard for me."

Playing with the Boys

Since girls' hockey leagues did not exist when she was young, Granato played on boys' hockey squads from kindergarten through junior high school. She was usually the only girl and often the youngest player on the ice, but her speed and skill made her a valuable player. "The boys didn't think it was the greatest thing to have a girl on their team, but they learned in time to respect me because they realized I could help the team," she recalled. "I have a feeling that if I hadn't been as successful at putting the puck away [scoring goals], the guys might not have been so crazy about having me as a teammate."

During her first years of junior hockey, Granato felt that she was treated like "one of the guys." But she recalls that "when I turned about 10 or 11 I couldn't change in the locker room with the boys anymore and that bothered me. That was such a raw deal for me. And other kids' parents would point fingers and whisper and tell their boys not to play with me. I didn't have as much trouble with my own team and my own league because everybody accepted my family. My mom tells me I would be in the women's bathroom changing and I'd say, 'I hate this. Why is everybody pointing fingers? Why is everybody saying stuff? And when I'd go on the ice it would all go away.'"

Once Granato reached middle school age, some opposing coaches and players were so bothered by her presence that they tried to drive her away from the game by physically punishing her. Granato refused to wilt, though. Years of rough play with her brothers had toughened her up. In addition, her team took steps to protect her from particularly unsportsmanlike conduct. For example, her coach occasionally told her to switch jersey numbers with one of the other players, and she often disguised herself by tucking her long hair up under her helmet.

> *During the winter, all the Granato children spent their days playing hockey on a pond across the street from their home. "We were on the pond all day. We'd come in for supper and sit at the table with our skates on and then go back across the street to play some more. Everything our family did was hockey, hockey, hockey."*

Granato's love for the game of hockey remained strong throughout this period. "The whole game is so exciting, so fast, so fun!" she once said. But the negative comments and abusive treatment eventually took their toll. "As Cammi got older and the boys she played against got bigger and stronger, it was tough because she was singled out and they tried to hurt her physically," recalled Natalie Granato. "She had quite a few serious injuries, like concussions, sprained shoulders, different things like that."

Time to Make a Change

One day, Granato's mother sat her daughter down for a difficult talk. "[She] tried to explain that my brothers could go somewhere in hockey but there wasn't much future in it for me," Cammi said. "She tried to talk me into playing another sport. I remember crying all day that day."

Granato reluctantly stopped playing organized hockey after her sophomore year in high school. "It was sad, but I had to get away from the game for a couple of years," she said. "The next level of hockey was all hitting and I wasn't into that part of the game, so I had to focus on other sports."

But despite this temporary retirement from the game, the exploits of her brothers continued to inspire Granato. In 1988, for example, she attended the Winter Olympics in Calgary, Alberta, to watch her brother Tony play on the USA team. "We were at the Opening Ceremony and . . . I couldn't stop bugging my mom," remarked Granato. "I said, 'I have to get here. I

Granato playing for Providence College, 1993.

want to get here. I want to be one of those athletes.'" Years later, she pointed to the 1988 Winter Olympics as a factor in her eventual return to hockey.
"The 1980 team [that defeated the Soviet hockey team] really did something to me, but when I got a chance to see my brother up close at the 1988
Games and I saw what a wonderful experience it was, I wanted to be part
of it," she said.

EDUCATION

Granato attended school in the Downers Grove public system. During her years at Downers Grove North High School, she emerged as a star basketball, soccer, and tennis player. In fact, she received both basketball and soccer scholarship offers from colleges during her senior year. In addition, Granato won silver and gold medals in team handball in 1989 and 1990 at the U.S. Olympic Festival, an amateur sports event that allows talented youngsters from all across the United States to compete in various Olympic sports.

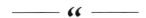

> *"Success follows Cammi like a shadow," said Providence University Coach John Marchetti. "Every time she touches the puck, something good happens. There are other players with great skills. Others may skate faster or shoot the puck better. But it all comes together for Cammi."*

Despite her many successes in these other sports, however, hockey continued to occupy a special place in Granato's heart. She sought out youth hockey tournaments for girls all across North America, where she often dominated the action. After one such tournament during her senior year, Providence University in Rhode Island offered her a scholarship to play hockey on the school's Lady Friars team. Granato quickly accepted, knowing that Providence was one of only three schools in the entire United States that offered scholarships to women hockey players at that time. In addition, Providence was a member of the East Coast Athletic Conference (ECAC), the only conference in the country that featured women's hockey. "I felt like I had betrayed hockey by not playing [in high school], and getting a scholarship to play hockey was a dream come true," she later said.

After earning her high school diploma in the spring of 1989, Granato headed to Providence. She thrived under the rules and style of women's hockey, which emphasized passing, puck handling, and goalmaking ability over checking and other punishing physical play. Granato tallied a hat trick — a three-goal game — in her very first college contest, and she capped her freshman season by earning conference rookie of the year honors.

Granato built on her fine freshmen performance, establishing herself as the conference's most dominant player in her final three years at Providence. She earned East Coast Athletic Conference player of the year honors in all three years (1991, 1992, and 1993), and in 1992 she set single-season school records for goals (48) and points (80). By the end of her four-year college career, Granato held school records for goals (139) and points (256) scored at Providence. Most importantly, she helped guide the Lady Friars to consecutive ECAC championships in 1992 and 1993. "Success follows Cammi like a shadow," said Providence Coach John Marchetti. "Every time she touches the puck, something good happens. There are other players with great skills. Others may skate faster or shoot the puck better. But it all comes together for Cammi." In the spring of 1993 Granato capped her terrific stint at Providence by earning a bachelor's degree in social science.

CAREER HIGHLIGHTS

At the same time that Granato skated for the Providence Lady Friars, she also became a cornerstone of the U.S. Women's National Team, which played in tournaments all over the world. She joined the team in 1990, when the International Ice Hockey Federation (IIHF) sponsored the first Women's World Ice Hockey Championship. Granato and her teammates advanced all the way to the gold medal round, only to lose to the heavily favored Canadian squad.

Granato remained a fixture on the USA team throughout the 1990s. In fact, she became the squad's leading scoring threat and almost always appeared at or near the top of the list of tournament scoring leaders. But despite the best efforts of Granato and her teammates, they finished second to Canada in each of the first four IIHF World Championships (1990, 1992, 1994, 1997). This string of silver medal finishes made Canada the focus of much of the American squad's preparation and training.

After graduating from Providence, Granato briefly coached a boys' youth hockey team in Wisconsin. But she then decided to attend graduate school at Concordia University in Montreal, Quebec. She knew that if she enrolled in a Canadian university she would be eligible to play sports for another four years. "When I got out of college, I had a lot of decisions to make," she recalled. "A lot of my friends were getting real jobs. I sat down with my parents and said financially [enrolling at Concordia] isn't the best situation for me, but this is something I want to do. Once I got their support, it was easy to make the decision, and it was the best decision I could have made. I had to make some sacrifices if I wanted to keep playing hockey. But deep inside I knew I had so much more hockey left to play."

Granato played for the Concordia Stingers from late 1993 through winter 1997. During that time, she amassed 179 career goals and 151 career assists. She also led the team in scoring in the 1995-1996 campaign, with an incredible 70 goals and 119 points in only 42 games. But her time at Concordia was marred by a frightening injury to her brother Tony during an NHL game. A violent collision in January 1996 left him with a life-threatening blood clot in his brain that required surgery. Fortunately, the operation went so well that he was able to return to professional hockey. But the close call made a deep impact on his sister. In the weeks following the injury, Granato played without her usual spirit and fearlessness. She later admitted that she had become frightened that a similar accident might happen to her. With encouragement from her brother, though, Granato gradually overcame her fears. By the end of the season, she was her old self again.

When the U.S. team won the first ever Olympic gold medals in women's hockey, the entire team screamed and jumped for joy. "To throw your gloves up and jump on the ice like that and celebrate and absolutely let go, that's a moment I will never, ever forget," recalled Granato. As the celebration continued, she spotted her family in the roaring crowd. "I could see the look in their eyes. I could see how proud they were."

Dreams of Olympic Glory

In 1997 Granato accepted an invitation to try out for Team USA's first ever women's Olympic hockey team. The International Olympic Committee (IOC), which is the Olympics' governing body, had approved women's hockey as a medal sport for the 1998 Olympics in Nagano, Japan. The idea that women's hockey would be played in the Olympics both surprised and excited Granato. "It was so hard to believe it was true," she recalled. "I was so excited to hear—it was the sport I worked at all my life. . . . The Olympics are as high as women can go in hockey. It will be our Stanley Cup."

Granato easily made the team. In fact, she was selected as captain of the squad in recognition of her hockey skills, leadership qualities, and high public profile. "She's definitely a pioneer," said teammate Sandra Whyte. "She's been fortunate enough to have media exposure and has used it well. She's been a great spokesperson, not only a great hockey player. She

Hockey teammates Granato (left) and Karyn Bye (right) show their gold medals following the U.S. win over Team Canada at the 1998 Olympics.

wants to spread the word that women's hockey is a great game and she's just an incredible role model."

Indeed, by this time Granato's performances in international competitions had made her America's best-known woman hockey player. She had even turned down a 1997 invitation from the NHL's New York Islanders to attend their training camp. She was flattered by the Islanders' offer, but she was much more interested in competing for a gold medal in the Olympics.

Early in 1997, Canada defeated the United States to claim yet another IIHF Women's World Ice Hockey Championship. But Granato and her teammates pointed out that they had nearly pulled off a big upset before falling 4-3 in overtime. "Each year we're closing the gap [between the teams]." said Granato. "Every year we're closer." As the year progressed, the American team whipped teams from Russia, Switzerland, and Finland in exhibition matches that served as warm-ups for the upcoming Olympics. But the most intense exhibitions were a 13-game series between the United States and Canada. These games, which were played in both countries, drew huge crowds and brought the rivalry between the two squads to new heights. When the dust settled, Canada had prevailed, winning 7 of the 13 contests.

But in December 1997—only two months before the Olympics—the U.S. team shut out the Canadians 3-0 in the finals of the Three Nations Cup, an event between the United States, Canada, and Finland. "We mentally know we can beat this team," Granato said afterward. "It's not as if there is a gap anymore."

In the days leading up to the Olympics, Granato recognized that a strong performance in the Games would give a big boost to American girls with aspirations of playing hockey or participating in other activities traditionally reserved for boys. "There are so many great stories about sacrifices and everything that goes into being an Olympian, and that's what we're about, too," she said. "Hopefully, people will get that into their minds and take a positive attitude about women's hockey, and get rid of the negative stereotypes, the people who say, 'You don't belong out there.'"

A Gold Medal Performance

Granato and her teammates traveled to Nagano, Japan, for the 1998 Winter Olympic Games. The hockey competition was set up as a round-robin tournament—a tournament in which every team plays every other team according to a set schedule. In Team USA's opening round game against China, Granato scored the first goal for the United States in Olympic women's hockey competition. The team subsequently rolled to a 5-0 shutout win, then defeated Sweden, Finland, and Japan to qualify for the gold medal game. But first, they had to play Canada—which had also qualified to play for the gold medal—in the final contest of the round-robin tournament. This clash was meaningless from a medal standpoint, but both teams attacked one another as if gold was on the line. In a penalty-riddled contest, Team USA eventually roared back from a 4-1 deficit to claim a 7-4 victory.

The stage was thus set for a rematch between the American and Canadian teams, with Olympic gold medals at stake. With her entire family watching, Granato skated out of the dressing room to fulfill her childhood dream of playing hockey in the Winter Olympics. The game turned out to be a tense, low-scoring affair, but Team USA managed to stake out a 2-0 lead with 10 minutes left. "It was the longest 10 minutes of my life," Granato later admitted. "I just wanted it to be over."

Canada mounted a desperate rally, but it fell short. When the final buzzer sounded, Granato and her teammates had clinched a 3-1 upset victory to claim the first ever Olympic gold medals in women's hockey. The entire American team screamed and jumped for joy as cheers rained down from supporters in the stands. "To throw your gloves up and jump on the ice like that and celebrate and absolutely let go, that's a moment I will never, ever forget," recalled Granato. As the celebration continued, she spotted her family in the roaring crowd. "I could see the look in their eyes," she said. "I could see how proud they were."

For Granato, winning Olympic gold was a "perfect" reward for her lifelong pursuit of hockey. "You play this game because you love it," she explained. "There's no money in it [for women]. There's no professional league. You're not going to be able to support yourself doing this. You go to college, and the guys tell you to get off the ice. But you keep plugging away, believing that there's a reason for all the work and time you put in. Then, all of a sudden, you're at the Olympics. And you've won. And everything you strived for has come true. And you cherish every second."

At the conclusion of the Olympics, Granato was given one more special Olympics memory. At that time, the American team captains from all the Olympic sports selected her to carry the American flag at the Games' closing ceremonies.

> "
>
> *"You play this game because you love it. There's no money in it [for women]. There's no professional league. You're not going to be able to support yourself doing this. You go to college, and the guys tell you to get off the ice. But you keep plugging away, believing that there's a reason for all the work and time you put in. Then, all of a sudden, you're at the Olympics. And you've won. And everything you strived for has come true. And you cherish every second."*
>
> "

Continuing in Hockey

In the weeks following the 1998 Olympics, Granato and her teammates appeared on television and in newspaper and magazine stories all across the country. She enjoyed the excitement and fuss, but knew that she would soon be returning to a more normal existence. In 1998 she accepted an offer to be the radio color commentator for the NHL's Los Angeles Kings, although her contract stipulated that she be allowed to continue playing women's hockey. "Right now, I'm trying to figure out how to balance everything," she said. "Lacing up my skates is second nature for me. Learning to call color takes a lot of effort and time. I have to refocus my goals and keep going. It is nice to have gold attached to [my] name, but there is more to life than an Olympic medal."

Granato shoots on German goalie Stephanie Wartosch-Kurten during the match between the U.S. and Germany at the 2002 Olympics. The U.S. shut out Germany, 10-0.

Granato remained on the U.S. National Team during this time. In fact, she continued to be a dominant performer, even though she was now playing with and against women who were 8 or 10 years younger than her. In 2000-2001 she ranked second on the team in scoring, and in 2001-2002 she led the team in scoring with 27 goals and 48 points in only 25 games. But she and her teammates found themselves once again coming up short against Canada's women's team. Canada defeated the United States to win three consecutive world championships in 1999, 2000, and 2001. These losses were enormously frustrating to Granato. "You can't get better than winning in the Olympics," she admitted. "But each year you work all season for the world championships, and then each year they win. You end up just looking at each other in a daze, saying 'When are we going to beat these guys?'"

Returning to the Olympics

Throughout this time, the team was preparing for the 2002 Winter Olympic Games, to be held in Salt Lake City, Utah. In the months before the

Olympics, Team USA finally seemed to be hitting on all cylinders. The squad won 20 consecutive matches, including eight in a row over their Canadian rivals. At most of these exhibitions against Canada, the American and Canadian squads stayed in the same hotel. But the two teams remained on very unfriendly terms. "There were no slumber parties," agreed Granato.

At the 2002 Olympics, the United States and Canada once again advanced through the tournament to the gold medal game. But this time, Canada stunned the favored U.S. team by a 3-2 score to win the championship. The loss forced Granato and the rest of the team to settle for a silver medal finish. "Any time you don't reach your goal, it's disappointing," Granato said afterward. "Losing really stings. Canada played great and deserved to win."

Since the 2002 Olympics ended, Granato has remained heavily involved in women's hockey. In May 2002 she agreed to play for the Vancouver Griffins, a team in the National Women's Hockey League (NWHL), an amateur league that features a number of North America's best women hockey players. "Cammi is one of the best players in the world and will have an immediate impact on our team," said Griffins' president Philip DeGrandpre. "She is a threat every time she is on the ice and leads by example."

In addition to playing for the Griffins, Granato hopes to represent her country in one more Olympics in 2006.

"Being successful in sports has given me independence and strength. I learned that I can be strong and impressive on the ice, yet feminine off the ice. . . . It's great to know that I can influence kids in the right way, in a positive way. It's always rewarding to talk to kids. I've visited a lot of schools and I know my teammates have too. The kids really do look up to us, and it's fun to let them try on the gold medal, see the sparkle in their eyes, answer a question about their sport or what they're trying to do. It makes them feel important. That's what I consider success."

"I'm not a spring chicken anymore but . . . I'm going to play to hopefully continue to be a part of the U.S. team and stay competitive," she said. But even if her days of Olympic competition are over, she is enormously grateful for the rewarding career that she has had. "Being successful in sports has given me independence and strength," she said. "I learned that I can

Granato (right) falls to the ice as she is tripped by Hanne Sikio of Finland during the 2002 Olympics.

be strong and impressive on the ice, yet feminine off the ice. Younger girls are not going to have to go through the same things that we went through. It's great to know that I can influence kids in the right way, in a positive way. It's always rewarding to talk to kids. I've visited a lot of schools and I know my teammates have too. The kids really do look up to us, and it's fun to let them try on the gold medal, see the sparkle in their eyes, answer a question about their sport or what they're trying to do. It makes them feel important. That's what I consider success."

HOME AND FAMILY

Granato lives in Vancouver, British Columbia. She is still unmarried, but she hopes eventually to raise a big family similar to the one in which she grew up.

HOBBIES AND OTHER INTERESTS

Granato enjoys a wide variety of athletic activities. In addition, she runs the Cammi Granato Gold Medal Hockey Camp for Girls. She and her family are also founders of the Golden Dreams for Children Foundation, which is dedicated to providing support to children with special needs.

HONORS AND AWARDS

Rookie of the Year, East Coast Athletic Conference: 1990
Player of the Year, East Coast Athletic Conference: 1991, 1992, 1993
USA Hockey Women's Player of the Year: 1996
Olympic Women's Hockey: 1998, Gold Medal; 2002, Silver Medal

FURTHER READING

Books

Lessa, Christina. *Women Who Win: Stories of Triumph in Sport and in Life,* 1998
Loverro, Thom. *Cammi Granato: Hockey Pioneer,* 2000 (juvenile)
Sports Stars, Series 5, 1999
Who's Who in America, 2002

Periodicals

Atlanta Journal-Constitution, Feb. 12, 2002, p.D7
Boston Globe, Feb. 7, 1998, p.G7
Chicago Tribune, Apr. 12, 1992, p.D1
Christian Science Monitor, Oct. 30, 1997, p.1
Current Biography Yearbook, 1998
Los Angeles Times, July 31, 1993, p.C4; Jan. 28, 1998, p.3; Nov. 5, 1998, p.6; Mar. 31, 1999, p.6
Newsday, Feb. 18, 1998, p.A78
People, Feb. 16, 1998, p.50
St. Louis Post-Dispatch, Feb. 6, 1998, p.D1
Sport, Apr. 1999, p.18
Sports Illustrated, Feb. 8, 1993, p.5; Apr. 21, 1997, p.130; Feb. 19, 2002, p.12
Sports Illustrated for Kids, Dec. 1996, p.70; Sep. 1, 2001, p.80
USA Today, Jan. 8, 1993, p.C10; July 30, 1993, p.C10; Jan. 26, 1998, p.C19; Apr. 7, 2000, p.C11; Feb. 20, 2002, p.D6; July 1, 2002, p.C3
Vancouver (B.C.) Sun, Sep. 3, 2002, p.C5

Online Articles

http://cnnsi.com
    (*CNN/Sports Illustrated,* "Golden Girls," Oct. 15, 1998)

http://teacher.scholastic.com/newszone/specialreports/olympics/athletes
 (*Scholastic*, "Cammi Granato," undated)

Online Databases

Biography Resource Center Online, 2002

ADDRESS

Cammi Granato
USA Hockey
1775 Bob Johnson Drive
Colorado Springs, CO 80906-4090

WORLD WIDE WEB SITES

http://www.granatohockey.com
http://www.olympic-usa.org
http://www.usahockey.com/usa_hockey/2002olympicswomens/2002
 olympicswomens

Chris Klug 1972-

American Professional Snowboard Racer
Winner of the Bronze Medal in Men's Parallel Giant
Slalom at the 2002 Winter Olympics
First Organ Transplant Recipient Ever to Win an
Olympic Medal

BIRTH

Christopher Jefferies Klug (pronounced *kloog*) was born on
November 18, 1972, in Vail, Colorado. His parents, Warren and
Kathy Klug, manage a resort hotel. Chris has an older brother,

Jim, and a younger sister, Hillary. He also has a foster brother, Jason Gillam, who came to live with the Klug family as a teenager.

YOUTH

Klug was born prematurely, before the lining of his lungs had developed fully. He caught pneumonia during his first few days of life and almost died. Pneumonia is an infection that causes the lungs to fill with fluid. But young Klug fought back and made a full recovery. The only lasting effect of this trauma was that he developed asthma as a boy.

Despite his early health problems, Klug was a happy and active child who enjoyed playing outdoors. His mother taught him to ski at Vail Mountain when he was two years old. The Klug family moved to Bend, Oregon, in 1976. Chris grew up skiing, hiking, and camping in the mountains, as well as riding his bicycle and skateboard.

Klug got his first snowboard as a Christmas present from his father in 1983, when he was 11 years old. The sport of snowboarding originated in the 1960s, when adventurous young people tried sliding down snow-covered hills on surfboards or on two skis bolted together. For many years, snowboarding was considered an "outlaw" sport and was not allowed at most ski resorts. But as the equipment improved and more trend-setting youngsters took up the sport, it rapidly gained in popularity and acceptance.

Klug developed an immediate love for snowboarding and began spending all his free time "shredding" on nearby Mt. Bachelor. "[I] began snowboarding in Moon Boots, of which the flex was determined by the number of wraps of duct tape," he recalled. "Riding powder with my friends and having fun were top priority. It's funny, that's still top priority! Mt. Bachelor was a mecca for shredders in the early years."

Starting to Compete

Within a few years, Klug began competing as an amateur in junior snowboarding competitions. He started out competing in all the major snowboarding events, including halfpipe, moguls, slalom, giant slalom, and super giant slalom (super G). In halfpipe events, snowboarders glide back and forth through a U-shaped tube, gaining speed on the downward slopes and performing tricks at the top of the upward slopes. In moguls competitions, snowboarders race down a hill covered with bumps and ramps made of snow.

Klug's favorite events were the slalom races, in which snowboarders race downhill and carve turns around a series of gates. The gates are progressively more widely spaced as competitors move from the slalom to the giant slalom and the super G. As a result, competitors in the super G achieve the fastest speeds, sometimes over 70 miles per hour. "I think competing in all of the disciplines early on in my snowboarding career really helped me develop as a strong, all-around rider," Klug noted.

Klug quickly moved from local snowboard races to the Northwest Race Series. He finished second in junior halfpipe at the North American Championship in 1987. The following year he placed second in both moguls and slalom at the U.S. Open. In 1989 he was named National Amateur Champion in slalom and super G.

EDUCATION

Despite all the time he spent practicing and traveling to snowboard races, Klug still did well in school and participated in team sports. In fact, he was an all-state quarterback at Mountain View High School in Bend, and he also played varsity tennis for the school. When he graduated from high school in 1991 with a 3.9 grade point average, he was recruited to play football at Oregon State University and several small colleges.

Klug began competing as a professional snowboarder while he was still in high school. Upon graduation, he faced a tough decision—whether to play college football or try to make a career in snowboarding. He spent 1992 at Deerfield Academy in Massachusetts, a prestigious prep school that would allow him to play one more year of high school football while also traveling on the professional snowboarding circuit. By the end of that year, he had decided to concentrate on snowboarding.

"[I] began snowboarding in Moon Boots, of which the flex was determined by the number of wraps of duct tape. Riding powder with my friends and having fun were top priority. It's funny, that's still top priority! Mt. Bachelor was a mecca for shredders in the early years."

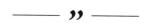

Klug plans to attend college when his snowboarding career is over. In 1995 he took classes at Colorado Mountain College in Aspen—where his family had moved in 1992—while he was recovering from surgery to correct bone problems in his heel. He also was accepted at Middlebury

College in Vermont, but he deferred admission until after the 2002 Winter Olympics.

CAREER HIGHLIGHTS

Racing in the 1998 Winter Olympics

Once he completed high school and dedicated himself to snowboarding full-time, Klug became a solid contender in international events. He finished eighth in the slalom in his first-ever World Cup event in Germany, and he chalked up four World Cup victories over the next few years. He also claimed five national championships and was the first snowboarder selected for the U.S. Olympic Team that would compete in the 1998 Winter Games in Nagano, Japan.

————— " —————

"In the early beginnings of the sport, a lot of people thought snowboarding had no place in the Olympics. They said the sport was all about soul, back-country riding, and freedom, that it wasn't about Olympic medals, fame, and fortune. But I've never felt that way. This is an exciting time for snowboarding. The Olympics is the ultimate in sports. It'll put us all on the map."

————— " —————

Klug was thrilled to participate in the first snowboard race ever held in the Olympics. He disagreed with the people who claimed that appearing in the Olympics would ruin the sport of snowboarding. "In the early beginnings of the sport, a lot of people thought snowboarding had no place in the Olympics," he explained. "They said the sport was all about soul, back-country riding, and freedom, that it wasn't about Olympic medals, fame, and fortune. But I've never felt that way. This is an exciting time for snowboarding. The Olympics is the ultimate in sports. It'll put us all on the map."

Olympic organizers chose to feature the giant slalom in the 1998 Games. Each competitor made two timed runs down the hill, and the athletes with the lowest combined times won medals. Klug posted an outstanding time in his first run and took second place, only .07 seconds behind the leader. But bad weather delayed the start of the second run. By the time he finally made his way down the hill, snow and thick fog made it difficult for him to see the course. Klug still started out strong, though, and at the halfway point the clock showed him in the lead by .15 seconds. But then he made

Klug competing in the men's giant slalom snowboarding event at the 1998 Olympics.

a slight error and caught his arm on one of the gates. The mistake slowed him down enough that he ended up finishing in sixth place, 1.29 seconds behind gold medalist Ross Rebagliati of Canada. "I guess I'm pleased to be sixth," Klug said later, "but it's all about medals when you come to the Olympics."

Despite his disappointing finish, Klug enjoyed his Olympic experience. "You can't really ask for a better first run for snowboarding. I'm thrilled for the sport. People all around the world will see what a great sport snow-boarding is. And they'll want to see more of it," he stated. "I have had a unique opportunity of being a part of snowboarding's evolution from wooden boards with bungee-strap bindings, and leashes that extended from the tip of the board to your front hand, to state-of-the-art equip-ment, and the arrival of snowboarding competition in the Olympic Games. Through all of this change, I still love to snowboard. This is why I continue to do it!"

Diagnosed with a Rare Liver Disease

It was later revealed that Klug had participated in the 1998 Olympics de-spite a serious health problem. Back in 1994, at the age of 21, Klug had undergone a routine medical examination in order to qualify for health insurance. His blood tests showed unusually high levels of enzymes coming from his liver. The liver is an organ that acts as the body's filtration system. It removes toxic chemicals, including drugs and alcohol, from the bloodstream. The liver also produces a fluid called bile that is carried through tubes called bile ducts to the small intestine, where it aids in digestion and nutrient absorption.

When doctors first noticed the unusual liver-enzyme numbers, they asked Klug if he used drugs or was a heavy drinker. He explained that he never used drugs and only had an occasional beer with his friends. Seeking another explanation, the doctors gave him a series of additional tests. It took them a year and a half to come up with a diagnosis. They finally told Klug that he had Primary Sclerosing Cholangitis (PSC), a rare disease in which the body's immune system attacks the bile ducts of the liver. The ducts gradually accumulate scar tissue until they no longer function. Then bile pools in the liver, causing infection and possibly liver cancer.

PSC affects one out of every 10,000 people in the United States. Most of its victims are young men. The cause of the disease is not known. Although the symptoms can be successfully treated for a while, there is no cure. Eventually people who have PSC must undergo a liver transplant, or else they will die. The doctors told Klug that he would need a liver transplant, but they could not tell him whether it would take three years or 30 years for his condition to progress to that level.

But a transplant would not necessarily be easy to achieve. In certain cases, when a person dies some of their organs can be removed and transplanted into someone else. But not many families make the difficult decision to donate organs at the painful moment when a loved one is dying. So there aren't enough organs available for transplant for all the people who need them. Those who need a transplant are placed on a national waiting list, and their placement on the list depends on the severity of their condition. Then they wait and hope for a call that a suitable organ is available. But there's no guaranty that an organ will become available in time.

Living with the Disease

When Klug was first diagnosed, he found it hard to believe that his liver was slowly failing. After all, he was an extremely healthy, highly conditioned athlete and could not have felt better. Following his diagnosis, he continued competing as a professional snowboard racer and participating in a number of other sports he enjoyed. Klug kept his condition secret from his fellow competitors and the media. He knew that many people thought of liver disease as something that affected alcoholics and drug addicts, and he wanted to maintain a clean reputation for both himself and his sport.

Klug had no symptoms of liver failure for the first four years after he was diagnosed with PSC. But he still had to see a doctor at regular intervals in order to have his bile ducts dilated (opened). In this procedure—which Klug referred to as a "roto-rooter"—the doctors would insert a special tube down his throat and guide it through his digestive tract to his liver. Klug started out having a roto-rooter procedure once a year, but he soon progressed to several times per year. Within a year of his appearance in the Olympic Games, he had to undergo the procedure once a month.

"They do this roto rooter treatment where they go in orally and dilate your bile ducts and try and open things up and get your plumbing working properly, but that's just a Band-Aid on the whole deal," Klug explained. "The bottom line was that things were just constricting and my bile ducts were shutting down and causing my liver to fail. The end result was I either continue that process—continue the scarring and end up with cancer and have no options—or they put a new pump in and I get to keep going."

"I was under the impression that PSC patients didn't die, and here's Walter Payton, one of the fittest, strongest, greatest football players ever, and he just died from this disease. I pulled over and started crying. It was the first time that it really hit me that I might die."

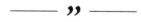

As the roto-rooter treatment became less effective, Klug's doctor placed him on the national list of people waiting for an organ transplant. At first Klug was angry at being put on the transplant list. He did not want to believe that his condition was that serious. But something happened in 1999 that helped him understand the situation he was facing.

Klug had long been a fan of Walter Payton, the legendary running back for the NFL's Chicago Bears. (For more information on Payton, see *Biography Today*, Jan. 2000.) His admiration for the football star only grew when Payton revealed in a press conference that he was suffering from PSC. A few months later, as Klug was driving from Aspen to Salt Lake City, Utah, for a training session, he heard on the radio that Payton had died of liver disease at the age of 45. "I was under the impression that PSC patients didn't die, and here's Walter Payton, one of the fittest, strongest, greatest football players ever, and he just died from this disease," Klug recalled. "I pulled over and started crying. It was the first time that it really hit me that I might die."

Undergoing a Liver Transplant

Klug continued competing on the professional snowboarding tour through the 1999 season. In fact, he was the top American on the World Cup circuit that year, with a victory at a World Cup race in Germany. He also won the U.S. national championship in 1999. Yet as the season concluded, Klug began showing unmistakable symptoms of liver failure. He often felt sick and got stabbing pains in his side. He also lost weight and ran a constant low-grade fever. By early 2000 the roto-rooter treatments were no longer effective in opening his bile ducts, and his doctors moved him up to the most urgent status on the organ transplant list.

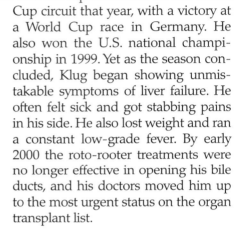

"Without a doubt the hardest part of the whole deal was the waiting game leading up to my transplant. It's not like a knee surgery. You can't just schedule it and get it fixed. I wore a pager every minute of the day and carried a cell phone as a backup in anticipation of receiving a call from the University Hospital Transplant Team informing me that a liver was available that matched my blood type and age."

Klug had to wait three months for a suitable liver to become available. During this time, he carried a pager everywhere he went so that his doctors would be able to reach him at a moment's notice. "Without a doubt the hardest part of the whole deal was the waiting game leading up to my transplant," he admitted. "It's not like a knee surgery. You can't just schedule it and get it fixed. I wore a pager every minute of the day and carried a cell phone as a backup in anticipation of receiving a call from the University Hospital Transplant Team informing me that a liver was available that matched my blood type and age."

During the summer of 2000, Klug grew steadily weaker as the bile pooled in his liver. He had to take strong antibiotics to keep infection from taking hold. On good days he still managed to ride his mountain bike or go waterskiing. But on bad days it was all he could do to lie on the couch and play chess. "I would get winded after doing one repetition [of weight lift-

Klug clears a gate during the men's parallel giant slalom at the 2002 Olympics.

ing]," he recalled. "It was pitiful. Every week I was getting a little bit sicker. I was pretty much bummed. I saw my dreams and everything passing."

The call finally came on July 28, 2000. Klug rushed to the airport in Aspen, but his flight to Denver was delayed by thunderstorms. He finally arrived at University Hospital, only to learn that his surgery had been postponed until the following morning so that doctors could find a recipient for the organ donor's heart. Klug spent six hours in surgery while the doctors removed his liver and replaced it with the healthy liver of a 13-year-old boy who had been shot in the head. The surgery left a long, Y-shaped scar

81

Klug slides across the top of the snow as he leans into a turn during the men's parallel giant slalom competition at the 2002 Olympics.

across his midsection. Thanks to his physical fitness, Klug recovered quickly from the operation and was able to leave the hospital in four days (the average stay for liver transplant patients is 12 days).

Following the successful liver transplant, Klug went public with his condition and expressed his gratitude to the family of the organ donor. "It was a miracle," he stated. "I'm lucky to be alive today. It was truly an amazing experience for me and for my family. To receive the gift of life is a humbling experience. I will forever be grateful for my second chance. Every day I thank God and I thank the individual's family for the decision to donate."

Making a Remarkable Comeback

Klug was determined to regain his physical conditioning and return to his career as a professional snowboard racer. His goal was to win a medal in the 2002 Winter Olympic Games, which were to be held in Salt Lake City, Utah. If he was successful, he would become the first organ transplant recipient ever to win an Olympic medal. He knew that such an accomplishment would bring him a great deal of attention, and he hoped to use that attention to raise public awareness of the need for organ donation.

In the month after his transplant surgery, Klug did a lot of walking and stationary biking. Then he returned to his home in Aspen and started an intensive program of physical therapy. "My abs [abdominal muscles] had been sliced through, so it took quite a while for them to come back and it left a 'bad' new tattoo," he noted. "I still get curious looks at the public pool or swimming hole when I shed my shirt for a dip. I've come up with some pretty good stories explaining my scar. The shark attack tale actually works!"

Klug took his first casual ride on a snowboard just two months after his surgery. At four months he returned to the World Cup circuit and posted one of his best seasons ever. Klug claimed his first post-transplant World Cup victory in January 2001. He attributed part of his success to his newfound focus and positive outlook. "An enormous weight had been lifted off of my shoulders and I was free to pursue my dreams once again," he recalled. "After fighting for my life and going through a liver transplant, going head to head in a parallel giant slalom on the World Cup Tour seemed easy. It put things in perspective for me once again. I realized how lucky I was to be out there doing what I loved to do, traveling the world on my snowboard."

Other than his scar and his new perspective, the main difference in Klug's life since the liver transplant has been the need to take anti-rejection medication. At several precise times each day, Klug must take expensive drugs that suppress his immune system in order to prevent his body from attacking his new liver. "In 90 percent of the cases, a transplant totally cures the condition [PSC] and you never have to deal with it again—aside from being pretty methodical about taking your drugs," he noted. "The more you're off with the drugs, the more you mess around, the better chance of having a rejection bout and having problems. I just don't mess with that. It doesn't limit me though. It's not like I have to sit at home and wait for noon to take my drugs. I just throw them in the cooler and we go surfing, we go wakeboarding, and if I go dirtbiking I just stick it in my back pocket and make sure I take it."

After the transplant, Klug says, "An enormous weight had been lifted off of my shoulders and I was free to pursue my dreams once again. After fighting for my life and going through a liver transplant, going head to head in a parallel giant slalom on the World Cup Tour seemed easy. It put things in perspective for me once again. I realized how lucky I was to be out there doing what I loved to do, traveling the world on my snowboard."

Klug's active lifestyle has led to several comic misadventures involving his anti-rejection medication. One time he carried a cooler containing his drugs onto a commercial airplane and placed it in the overhead bin. But the ice melted and started leaking down onto the heads of the passengers below. Another time Klug left his drugs in his hotel room for safekeeping. But the hotel maid went overboard while cleaning the room and threw them out. Klug and his friends ended up digging through a snowbank in the hotel parking lot in order to find them.

"Being on the organ waiting list was a very scary place to be, but I was very fortunate not to be one of the 16 people who die every day while waiting for an organ transplant. No one should have to be on the waiting list. My goal is to eliminate the organ donor waiting list — to make that list a thing of the past."

Winning the Bronze Medal in the 2002 Olympics

Klug performed well enough during the 2002 season to qualify for the U.S. Olympic Team. He was honored when his teammates selected him to play a special role in the opening ceremony of the Winter Olympic Games in Salt Lake City, Utah. Klug was one of the athletes who carried an American flag that had been found in the debris of the World Trade Center following the terrorist attacks of September 11, 2001. "It was one of the coolest things I've ever been able to do, definitely a tremendous honor," he said afterward. "It was pretty powerful too, holding that flag and the wind was blowing through it and it's all tattered and scorched and burned. It was very moving. I felt my knees wobbling a few times."

Klug's event for the 2002 Olympics was the parallel giant slalom. This event is basically the same as a giant slalom race, except that there are two parallel sets of gates on the hill and two competitors race at the same time. All the racers participate in a timed qualifying round, and the 16 riders with the lowest times advance to the next round. These 16 competitors race in a series of head-to-head match-ups based on their qualifying positions (for example, the top rider races against the rider ranked 16th, and so on). Each pair of riders makes two runs through the course, and the rider who wins both runs or has the lowest combined time advances to the next round. "It's a little bit of mental warfare and riding strategy," Klug ex-

Klug (right) and Nicholas Huet of France (left) race down the course.

plained. "It's very, very spectator friendly. It makes my job a little harder, but it's a lot of fun for the spectator."

Klug placed 11th in the qualifying run and fought his way to the semifinals, in which the final four competitors race to determine who wins the Olympic medals. Klug ended up racing for the bronze medal against Nicholas Huet of France. Klug won the first of their two runs, but he broke a buckle on his boot in the process. He did not have time to change his boots, so a friend did a makeshift repair job using a piece of wire and some duct tape. "It was only appropriate," Klug joked. "I started with moon boots and duct tape 19 years ago, so it was the right solution." Despite the broken buckle, Klug won the second run to claim the bronze medal. Philipp Schoch of Switzerland won the gold, and Richard Richardsson of Sweden took the silver.

Klug was so excited when he won the bronze medal that he jumped over a snow fence to join the crowd of friends and family members cheering him on. His achievement helped the American team win a record 34 medals in the 2002 Games. The fact that he had earned his medal just 18 months after undergoing a liver transplant made it even more impressive. "With this medal," said his doctor, Greg Everson, "Chris has proven that, for people with severe chronic illnesses, the promise for the future is so very great."

The medals ceremony for the men's parallel giant slalom: gold medal winner Philipp Schoch of Switzerland (center) is flanked by silver medal winner Richard Richardsson of Sweden (left) and bronze medal winner Klug (right).

Promoting Organ Donation

As he expected, Klug received a great deal of attention following his performance in the Olympic Games. He was interviewed for many newspapers, magazines, and television programs. In addition, he was included among the Sexiest Men in Sports of 2002 by the editors of *Sports Illustrated Women*. He also made endorsement deals with Hershey's chocolate milk and Mr. Coffee. Finally, the U.S. Olympic Committee honored him with its 2002 Olympic Spirit Award.

Klug used all the media attention to spread his message about the importance of organ donation. He noted that advances in medical technology have made organ transplants a life-saving option for more people. But this has created a serious shortage of donors to provide organs for transplant. In fact, there were more than 80,000 individuals on the waiting list for organ transplants in the United States in 2002. About 63 people receive transplants across the country each day, but another 16 people die before a suitable organ becomes available. "Being on the organ waiting list was a very scary place to be, but I was very fortunate not to be one of the 16 people who die every day while waiting for an organ transplant," Klug stated. "No one should have to be on the waiting list. My goal is to eliminate the organ donor waiting list—to make that list a thing of the past." He encourages people to sign the organ donation stickers on their driver's licenses, register with central organ banks in states where they exist, and inform their families of their wish to donate organs.

Klug feels that his liver transplant has made him a better person. "I look down and I've got this tattoo going all the way across my midsection from the surgery, and it blows me away. I'll never forget it," he said. "By the same token, I wouldn't have traded that transplant experience for anything. . . . Without a doubt, I don't take a single curveside or hillside turn on my snowboard for granted. I love being out there and I love it more than ever."

———— **"** ————

"I look down and I've got this tattoo going all the way across my midsection from the surgery, and it blows me away. I'll never forget it. By the same token, I wouldn't have traded that transplant experience for anything. . . . Without a doubt, I don't take a single curveside or hillside turn on my snowboard for granted. I love being out there and I love it more than ever."

———— **"** ————

HOME AND FAMILY

Klug divides his time between homes in Aspen, Colorado, and Sisters, Oregon. He is not married, though he has been dating Melissa (Missy) April for more than 10 years. They met in high school, when they were members of rival tennis teams. April teaches special education classes in Aspen.

HOBBIES AND OTHER INTERESTS

Klug enjoys all kinds of sports, including surfing, waterskiing, mountain biking, tennis, and golf. He also plays the guitar and is a big fan of reggae legend Bob Marley. He spends his free time promoting organ donation and holding snowboard racing camps for kids.

HONORS AND AWARDS

Olympic Snowboarding, Giant Slalom: 1998, Sixth Place
Olympic Snowboarding, Parallel Giant Slalom: 2002, Bronze Medal
Olympic Spirit Award (U.S. Olympic Committee): 2002

FURTHER READING

Periodicals

Boys' Life, Jan. 2002, p.28
Chicago Tribune, Dec. 29, 2001, Sports sec., p.1
Denver Westword, Mar. 8, 2001; Mar. 15, 2001
Los Angeles Times, Jan. 26, 2002, p.A1
New York Daily News, Feb. 8, 1998, p.54
New York Times, Dec. 25, 2001, p.S1
Newsday, Jan. 15, 2002, p.B6
People, Dec. 3, 2001, p.141
Rocky Mountain News, Nov. 6, 2001, p.D3; Feb. 16, 2002, p.S6
Salt Lake Tribune, Oct. 24, 2000, p.A1
San Francisco Chronicle, Dec. 25, 2001, p.C1
Sports Illustrated, Feb. 14, 2002, p.10
USA Today, Feb. 3, 1998, p.C6; Dec. 7, 2000, p.C9; Feb. 16, 2002, Bonus sec.,
    p.3

Online Articles

http://snowboard.mountainzone.com/interviews/2000/klug/html
    (*Mountainzone.com,* "Q & A Session with Chris Klug,"undated)
http://teacher.scholasic.com/newszone/specialreports/olympics/athletes/
    klug.htm (*Scholastic,* "Chris Klug,"undated)
http://www.snowboardnetwork.com/articles/chrisklugtransplant.htm
    (*Snowboardnetwork.com,* "Olympic Snowboarder Undergoes Successful
    Liver Transplant,"July 28, 2000)
http://www.bomberonline.com/Bomber_Files/Chris_Klug/chris_klug.html
    (*Bomberonline.com,* "Chris Klug Interview,"Mar. 29, 2002)

ADDRESS

Chris Klug
U.S. Ski and Snowboard Association
P.O. Box 100
Park City, UT 84060

WORLD WIDE WEB SITES

http://www.chrisklug.com
http://www.olympic-usa.org/athlete_profiles/c_klug.htm

Jonny Moseley 1975-

American Freestyle Skier
Winner of the Gold Medal in Men's Moguls at the
1998 Winter Olympics

BIRTH

Jonny Moseley was born on August 27, 1975, in San Juan, Puerto Rico, but his family moved to the San Francisco area when he was a child. His father is Tom Moseley, a prominent developer and contractor who has built a number of prestigious yacht club facilities in California. His mother, Barbara, is a real estate broker in the San Francisco Bay area. Moseley has two older brothers, Rick and Jeff.

YOUTH

Moseley grew up in Tiburon, California, as part of a wealthy family that loved the outdoors. His father was an active and athletic man who passed down his passion for sailing and downhill skiing to all three of his sons. Looking back on his early years, Moseley recalled that he seemed to spend entire summers cruising on the Pacific Ocean, while most winter weekends involved repeated charges down the slopes of ski resorts tucked high in the Sierra Nevada Mountains. "It was a rough life, but I dealt with it OK," he joked.

"I always wanted to be the best. I think competition is key. At an early age, because my brothers used to work me, I realized what competition did, how it made me feel. I realized what it meant to me. I love the feeling of winning."

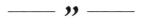

Moseley was first introduced to downhill skiing at the age of four by his father. The young boy's boldness, enthusiasm, and athletic ability enabled him to develop his talents quickly. By the age of ten, Moseley was a member of the freestyle ski club at California's beautiful but challenging Squaw Valley resort.

During his early years Moseley concentrated on alpine skiing, in which skiers slalom downhill. But he eventually became bored with alpine and decided to move on to competitive freestyle skiing. His specialty became moguls skiing. In this type of skiing, participants race down a slope that is dotted with large "moguls" (mounds of snow). As they navigate the moguls, they also perform two tricks in the air at jumps located one-third and two-thirds of the way down the slope. The final scores in freestyle events are determined by the speed of the downhill run and the quality of the jumps, measured in terms of height, form, and artistic value.

By his early teens, Moseley recognized that he was an unusually gifted skier. He later attributed his progress not only to his superior physical abilities in areas like strength, speed, and coordination, but also to a strong competitive drive. "I always wanted to be the best," he said. "I think competition is key. At an early age, because my brothers used to work me, I realized what competition did, how it made me feel. I realized what it meant to me. I love the feeling of winning."

At age 15 Moseley won the junior nationals skiing championship held in Lake Placid, New York. This triumph became a significant turning point in his life. "What I found out about myself [at the junior nationals] was that I was good at competing, not just skiing," Moseley recalled. "I loved that feeling. I liked being in the gate, all jacked up, nervous. I actually liked that feeling. . . . And when I found out about winning, I liked the competition even more."

Over the next few years, the teen sensation proved that his championship at Lake Placid was no fluke. "When I was 16 I won junior nationals again," Moseley remembered. "Then next I won junior nationals and North American amateurs; I mean, I won everything in sight. For a couple of years there I was getting way better, I was getting awesome. And when I made the U.S. Ski Team, I realized I could get paid to ski."

EDUCATION

Moseley attended high school at San Francisco's prestigious Branson School. During the school year he spent many weekends training or competing on distant race courses. Yet he still found time to post solid grades, star on the school's baseball and soccer teams, and perform in high school theatrical productions of *Oklahoma!* and *Our Town*. "The drama teacher at school always pulled me out of soccer practice and put me in the plays," according to Moseley. "I didn't even audition. I thought, 'Drama? I'm a jock!' But I did it, and it started the seed in me to perform and light up when I get in front of an audience."

After earning his diploma from Branson, Moseley enrolled at the University of California-Davis. He spent the next three years trying to balance classwork with his heavy training and competition schedule. His outgoing and friendly nature made this task even more difficult, for he greatly enjoyed partying and socializing with his friends. He finally dropped out at the end of his junior year in order to focus on his skiing career. But Moseley insists that he intends to return to college and earn his bachelor's degree after his career in competitive skiing are over.

CAREER HIGHLIGHTS

Moseley joined the top ranks of freestyle skiing in 1994. As a member of the World Cup circuit, he traveled to events all across North America and Europe. In his first few World Cup events, he admits that he "just got smoked" by the other skiers. But he steadily improved, and at the end of the season he was named Rookie of the Year by the FIS (Federation International de Ski).

In 1995 and 1996 Moseley emerged as a major name in international freestyle skiing. He earned a bronze medal at the 1995 World Cup Championships in La Clusaz, France, and the following year he claimed the overall World Cup Championship. These successes firmly established him as the top moguls skier in the United States. But friends and family insisted that the handsome skier never let his success go to his head. "He is really cool about who he is," said fellow skier Shane Anderson. "And he doesn't have to act big to make sure you know he's a big deal."

Despite his quick ascent to the top of America's skiing world, though, Moseley knew there was room for improvement. As the 1998 Winter Olympics approached, he worked closely with his coaches to improve his skiing technique and hone his mental toughness. "We discovered that for me there was a difference between stress and pressure," he explained. "Stress is when you're out on the hill training and you're doing your best runs and you look up and you know there's some other dude out there that's got mad skills that are better than you. There's no way you can be relaxed and try to compete well when you're under stress. But pressure is when you know you have the skills, when you know you can win, but you got gnarly butterflies. Then it's just a matter of turning that into *power*, you know, just going for it and letting it flow."

> "[For] me there was a difference between stress and pressure. Stress is when you're out on the hill training and you're doing your best runs and you look up and you know there's some other dude out there that's got mad skills that are better than you. There's no way you can be relaxed and try to compete well when you're under stress. But pressure is when you know you have the skills, when you know you can win, but you got gnarly butterflies. Then it's just a matter of turning that into **power**, you know, just going for it and letting it flow."

As the 1997-98 World Cup season unfolded, Moseley continued to perform at a dominant level. By season's end he had claimed the U.S. Men's Freestyle Championship, the World Cup Overall Standings Championship, and a gold medal finish in the World Cup Championships. But despite all these successes, Moseley felt that his standout season would be incomplete without an Olympic gold medal.

Moseley at the 1998 Olympics.

The 1998 Olympics

Moseley traveled to Nagano, Japan, for the 1998 Winter Olympic Games. As he prepared for the men's moguls event, the normally sociable skier shut himself off from friends and family in order to focus on the upcoming battle for Olympic gold. "I was concerned about keeping my stomach in my body," he admitted. "My mother didn't quite understand, but I figured I had to sacrifice to get the big one."

When the day for the men's moguls arrived, Moseley did not disappoint. He easily qualified for the medal round, cruising effortlessly down the course. Then, in the finals, he unveiled a terrific performance highlighted by a bold jump borrowed from the worlds of skateboarding and snowboarding. Midway through his run, he executed a daring "360 mutegrab" —a jump in which he completed a 360-degree spin in mid-air while simultaneously crossing his skis and holding them with one hand. "The 360 mute-grab, it's just a skiing helicopter," Moseley later explained. "But I just took some large air and when I got backwards I just grabbed the inside ski and tweaked it so it looks big, and there was a big crossed skis in the back. And it was just a beautiful photography shot with a crowd in the back, and I really did it so I could see the whole crowd as I went around. Because I really wanted to see where I was. So I did a 360 so I could check it out. And it was exciting, and the crowd loved it, and so did the judges." Moseley finished the maneuver with a perfect landing, then cruised across the finish line to claim his first Olympic gold medal. "[Winning the gold medal is] the best feeling of my life," he said. A short time later, Moseley learned that his gold medal was the first one earned by an American in the 1998 Winter Games.

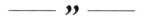

> *"The 360 mute-grab, it's just a skiing helicopter. But I just took some large air and when I got backwards I just grabbed the inside ski and tweaked it so it looks big, and there was a big crossed skis in the back. And it was just a beautiful photography shot with a crowd in the back, and I really did it so I could see the whole crowd as I went around. Because I really wanted to see where I was. So I did a 360 so I could check it out. And it was exciting, and the crowd loved it, and so did the judges."*

When Moseley received his gold medal a few hours later, he admitted that the ceremony tugged at his emotions. "It was a great feeling of accomplishment, being at the top of the podium, you know?" he said. "The crowd [for the medal ceremony] was so packed. And I could see on the left, up on the deck [were] my parents and all my family and all my friends. And I could hear them screaming. . . . And when they played the National Anthem, that was just the icing [on the cake], you know, to actually be in a position where you're listening to your National Anthem after winning a gold medal for your country."

Moseley doing the 360 mute-grab during the men's moguls competition at the 1998 Olympics.

A New Level of Fame

Moseley's exciting gold medal run made him one of the hottest stories of the Olympic Games. *Skiing* magazine called him "a California boy with the skills of a champion, the lingo of a surfer, and an irreverent, irrepressible spirit [who] uncorked something fresh and hip—and captured Olympic gold in the process." In addition, he appeared on television shows ranging from "The Today Show" to "Oprah" to "Late Night with David Letterman" and gave dozens of interviews to newspapers, magazines, and radio shows.

"I knew there would be a certain amount of fame and celebrity, but the way people in America responded was something I don't think anyone expected," Moseley stated.

Moseley was even asked to participate in a nationally televised *Superstars* competition in the summer of 1998. This event pitted him against an assortment of stars from other sports, including NFL stars Keyshawn Johnson, Kordell Stewart, Jason Sehorn, and Herschel Walker, heavyweight boxer Lennox Lewis, and long jump world record holder Mike Powell. "When I first got there, I think [the other athletes] thought I was a cameraman or maybe someone to tune up the jet skis," said Moseley. "Then I won the kayak event and was second in the swim. Keyshawn Johnson started talking like, 'Hey, this is a white guy's event.' And then we did golf and biking and jet skiing and he's saying, 'Well, yeah, he can win as long as there's *equipment* involved.'" But in the obstacle course event, Moseley silenced Johnson once and for all by scorching Stewart and claiming second place. The laid-back skier ended up claiming second place both in the obstacle course and the overall competition, behind only Sehorn.

> ―――― " ――――
>
> *"I just never envisioned [competing] past '98 in the first place. For me after '98 it wasn't a question if I could take two years off. It was not a choice. I was done. I couldn't swallow another competition. . . . The amount of effort, the amount of energy that went into winning the gold medal was too much to fathom doing again at that time."*
>
> ―――― " ――――

Moseley found that his sudden celebrity status did have some drawbacks. "I have to make extra efforts to be like who I was, because I like who I was," he admitted. "I had no problems with who I was. Now, I have to plan time to ski alone or with my friends. When I'm at home, I need to make sure to call my good friends and be with my family. I almost, like, have to recall who I was, and then make an effort to be that way."

But when he weighed all the advantages and disadvantages of his life after his gold medal performance, Moseley freely acknowledges that he enjoyed himself immensely. "I sucked the life out of my fame, took it to the limit," he said. "I worked that gold medal to the limit. For me, that meant being America's guest. I went to every party. I did every show. It was a dream. I took advantage of all of it. I don't regret it."

Indeed, Moseley's many television appearances and promotional obligations contributed to a two-year absence from international skiing competition after Nagano. "I just never envisioned [competing] past '98 in the first place," he later said. "For me after '98 it wasn't a question if I could take two years off. It was not a choice. I was done. I couldn't swallow another competition. . . . The amount of effort, the amount of energy that went into winning the gold medal was too much to fathom doing again at that time."

Trying for Another Olympic Shot

Moseley's decision to skip two World Cup seasons forced the U.S. ski team to drop him from their roster. At first, the ski team's decision angered the young star. "In the beginning I was really offended by the ski team," he admitted. "Why couldn't I just walk back into the Olympics? I just wanted to show up in the gate and defend my title. It took a year to kind of quell that cockiness and come back to the normal level of not only being an equal on the team but kind of being an underdog."

In 2001, in his first World Cup event in more than two years, Moseley finished dead last in the competition and hurt his back during one run. This woeful performance was hard for him to take, considering that he had won 17 World Cup events back in the mid- to late-1990s. As he struggled to regain his old form, Moseley remembered that "I was getting pretty discouraged. I knew I still had the skills and technique to win. In a lot of ways, I trained almost harder than in 1998. But I'd feel like I'd put down a good run and boom! — I'd finish 19th or 20th."

Moseley persevered, however, and late in the season he finally earned a silver medal at a World Cup event held at Sunday River, Maine. "That one [performance] gave me the notion that I wasn't completely washed up," Moseley recalled. "I started to believe I could win and get back to the Olympics." In late 2001 he still appeared to be a longshot to make the team for the 2002 Winter Olympics in Salt Lake City, Utah. But in January 2002 Moseley won a World Cup event in France. The triumph gave him just enough points to secure a spot on the team. Still, he entered the 2002 Olympics as the United States' lowest-ranked moguls skier.

As the Winter Games approached, Moseley decided that he wanted to shake up the freestyle skiing establishment. Like many other young skiers, he was unhappy that some of the wild and spectacular jumps that had been developed over the previous few years were forbidden under the moguls rules issued by the sport's governing body, the FIS (Federation International de Ski). For example, FIS rules say that if a competitor's head

*Moseley doing the dinner roll in the men's moguls competition
at the 2002 Olympics.*

goes below his feet during a jumping maneuver, he is automatically disqualified. Moseley and other skiers believed that these restrictions greatly limited the appeal and creativity of the sport. "This sport used to be judged on its 'wow' factor," said Moseley. "Someone did something and the judges would say: 'How did you like that? Was that cool or unique?' But it's not the overall impression of something anymore. It's what's expected instead. Which makes everyone start to do the same tricks following the winner. Where's the free in freestyle?"

Moseley subsequently declared his intention to perform a controversial maneuver called the "dinner roll" in the freestyle moguls event. He thought that by performing this aerial trick, in which the skier completes two full rotations in midair while keeping his body horizontal to the ground, he might be able to spark some changes in the scoring of freestyle skiing. "I want to win, but I try to win in the same fashion I won the last one—with something unique, exciting, and new," he said. "I'm either going to win or I'm not going to [earn a medal]. I'm not going for second. I definitely don't want to walk around trying to explain how I did this really cool trick and the judges didn't score it. But I'm not going to cater to what I think they're going to score. It's a great trick. The crowd loves it. . . . I feel like I can throw it and ski away. It's in the judges' hands now."

> *"This sport used to be judged on its 'wow' factor. Someone did something and the judges would say: 'How did you like that? Was that cool or unique?' But it's not the overall impression of something anymore. It's what's expected instead. Which makes everyone start to do the same tricks following the winner. Where's the free in freestyle?"*

Serving Up a Dinner Roll

When Moseley performed the dinner roll in his qualifying run, the crowd cheered appreciatively. But the spotlight did not really fall on him until his medal round run. When Moseley's turn came, he flew down the slopes as the crowd of 14,000 spectators urged him on. Midway through his run, he delivered the dinner roll as promised. He soared into the air, twisting and rotating two full revolutions in the air with his body horizontal to the ground before coming down to the slope for a perfect landing. The crowd cheered wildly, clanging cowbells and waving flags in appreciation of his spectacular trick. But despite the perfect execution of the trick move and the obvious delight of the fans, Moseley finished just out of the medal hunt with a fourth-place finish. The winner of the event was Janne Lahtela of Finland, who performed two solid aerial tricks and posted the fastest downhill time of all the competitors. When asked about Moseley's dinner roll, Lahtela shrugged and said, "You have to have more than one jump in a race to win." But he added that "This is show business and you have to please the people. What Jonny is doing for the sport is good."

———— " ————

After the 2002 Olympics, Moseley had this to say about not winning a medal: "Obviously, everyone wants to get the medal. I would have ideally liked to have done the trick and win or get in the top three. But I'm very satisfied with what I wanted to do. . . . People who know the sport will consider me very bold and legendary. Those who don't will see fourth place and say 'Oh, he screwed up.'"

———— " ————

For his part, Moseley insisted that he was "very, very pleased" with his showing. "Obviously, everyone wants to get the medal," he admitted. "I would have ideally liked to have done the trick and win or get in the top three. But I'm very satisfied with what I wanted to do. . . . People who know the sport will consider me very bold and legendary. Those who don't will see fourth place and say 'Oh, he screwed up.'"

Still Having Fun

In the weeks following the close of the 2002 Winter Games, Moseley continued to enjoy the trappings of stardom. He hosted an episode of "Saturday Night Live" and even accepted an invitation to give the commencement address to graduating seniors at the University of California's Berkeley campus. Some Berkeley students expressed anger and disappointment at the selection of Moseley, a college dropout. But a representative of the school's selection committee explained that "this class wanted to hear about living a life of commitment to your goals. A gold medalist represents the values of working hard and striving to be the best at what you do." For his part, Moseley refused to be drawn into the controversy. Instead, he gave a speech in which he poked fun at himself and urged the graduates to define success in accordance with their own personal values. "If you do not depend on awards, money, or other validations to dictate your well-being and your measure of success, you will own your own happiness," he said.

Moseley is not certain how long he will continue with his skiing career. In fact, he has expressed interest in competitive sailing, a sport in which both of his brothers are involved. "I grew up sailing," he reminds people, "and I love it from a tactical point of view. It's like skiing except you can do it with your buddies. There's a lot of fun to be had. And like skiers, sailors have really good parties. It also takes you to some of the most beautiful places in the world. I love the mountains, but I have an affinity for the sea."

HOME AND FAMILY

Moseley lives in a three-bedroom apartment in Tiburon, California, outside of San Francisco. But he spends little time there because he travels so frequently. "I like to be able to live out of just four duffel bags," he said.

HOBBIES AND OTHER INTERESTS

In addition to skiing and sailing, Moseley enjoys waterskiing, wakeboarding, and fixing up old cars.

HONORS AND AWARDS

Junior National Champion, freestyle moguls: 1991, 1992, 1993
Rookie of the Year (Federation International de Ski): 1994
World Cup Champion, Overall, freestyle moguls: 1996, 1998
World Cup Championships, freestyle moguls: 1998, Gold Medal
U.S. Champion, freestyle moguls: 1998
Olympic Freestyle Moguls: 1998, Gold Medal
U.S. Olympic Committee Sportsman of the Year: 1998
Beck International Award (U.S. Ski Team): 1998, for outstanding perfor-
    mance in international competition
Winter X-Games: 2000, Big Air Silver Medal
Gravity Games: 2000, Big Air Silver Medal

FURTHER READING

Books

Who's Who in America, 2000

Periodicals

Atlanta Journal-Constitution, Feb. 13, 2002, p.C5
Boston Globe, Apr. 2, 1998, p.D11; Jan. 31, 1999, magazine section, p.8
Boston Herald, Feb. 13, 2002, p.109

Boys' Life, Feb. 1999, p.14
Denver Rocky Mountain News, Nov. 24, 1998, p.C16; Jan. 18, 2002, p.C13
Freeskier Magazine, Feb. 2002
Los Angeles Times, Feb. 13, 2002, p.U3
New York Times, Feb. 11, 1998, p.C1; Dec. 4, 2001, p.S6; Feb. 11, 2002, p.D9;
    Feb. 13, 2002, p.D2; May 19, 2002, p.L10
Outside, Sep. 1998, p.68
People, June 24, 2002, p.108
Philadelphia Inquirer, Feb. 12, 2002, p.E9
Sacramento Bee, May 18, 2002, p.A3
San Francisco Chronicle, May 6, 2001, p.B3; Feb. 13, 2002, p.C1; May 18,
    2002, p.A17
San Francisco Examiner, Feb. 5, 1998, p.D3
Seventeen, Aug. 1998, p.214
Skiing, Sep. 1998, p.66; Dec. 1999, p.78
Sports Illustrated, May 20, 2002, p.22
Time International, Feb. 25, 2002, p.49
USA Today, Feb. 11, 1998, p.E9; Feb. 12, 1998, p.E10; Dec. 3, 1998, p.E4; Sep.
    6, 2001, p.C8

Online Articles

http://www.skiingmag.com
    (*Skiingmag.com,* "U.S. Freestyle Team: Jonny Moseley,"Winter 2001-2002)

Online Databases

Biography Resource Center, 2002, article from *The Complete Marquis Who's
    Who*

ADDRESS

Jonny Moseley
U.S. Ski and Snowboard Association
P.O. Box 100
Park City, Utah 84060

WORLD WIDE WEB SITES

http://www.johnnymoseley.com
http://internal.ussa.org/PR/public/Biosfre.asp?ussaid=4369799
http://www.olympic-usa.org/athlete_profiles/j_moseley.html

Apolo Ohno 1982-
American Speedskater
Winner of Gold and Silver Medals at the 2002 Winter
Olympics

BIRTH

Apolo Anton Ohno was born on May 22, 1982, in Seattle,
Washington. His father is Yuki Ohno, a hairdresser who owns
his own salon in the Seattle area. An immigrant from Japan,
Yuki Ohno combined words from the Greek language to name
his son. Apolo's first name means "to lead away" and his middle name means "priceless" in Greek. Apolo Ohno's mother is

Jerrie Lee, but she and Yuki Ohno divorced shortly after their son was born. She promptly disappeared from her son's life, leaving Ohno's father to raise him by himself. Since that time, Apolo Ohno has had no contact with his mother. Ohno also has an older half-brother, but they do not have a close relationship.

YOUTH

Ohno grew up in Federal Way, Washington, a suburb of Seattle. During Apolo's childhood, his father emphasized discipline, respect, and hard work in raising his son. But he also made special efforts to provide Apolo with outlets for his youthful energy. For example, they spent many weekends at cabins that looked out on the Pacific Ocean. On these trips, they passed their afternoons exploring rocky trails that wound through thick forests or prowling sandy beaches for seashells and other treasures. In addition, Yuki Ohno encouraged his son's early interest in swimming and inline skating, also known as rollerblading.

> *By age 14, Ohno was openly rebelling against his father and other authority figures. "If my dad said yes, I said no. That's the way it was for years. . . . There were times I'd go spend the night at a friend's house, and I wouldn't come home until like three days later."*

But despite his father's deep love for Ohno, the demands of his business often kept him away from home from early morning until evening. As a result, Apolo—who was nicknamed "Chunky" by his childhood chums—was taking care of himself after school by the time he was eight years old. On some evenings, he completed his homework, made dinner, and put himself to bed before his father even pulled in the driveway. Ohno recognized that his father loved him deeply, even if he rarely was home for dinner. But his father's absences also made the boy more reliant on his friends for companionship.

By the time Ohno reached middle school, he had blossomed into an extremely talented young athlete. A top-notch swimmer, he earned a state championship in the breaststroke when he was 12 years old. In addition, he had developed his inline skating skills to the point that he was routinely winning regional competitions in his age group. But in 1994 a new sport dazzled the youngster, prompting him to leave swimming and rollerblading behind.

A Speedskating Phenomenon

Like many other American families, Apolo Ohno and his father were glued to the television for much of the 1994 Winter Olympics. One night, young Ohno happened to be watching during coverage of the Olympic short track speedskating event. He was captivated by the event, which had only been introduced to the Olympics two years earlier, at the 1992 Games in Albertville, France. Until that time, both the Winter and the Summer Olympic Games took place in the same year, every four years. After 1992, the two sets of games were staggered, with the Winter Games in 1994 (and every four years thereafter) and the Summer Games in 1996 (and every four years thereafter).

In short track speedskating, athletes compete against each other instead of a clock on a standard 400-meter oval ice track. They race counterclockwise in groups of four, and racers can pass each other at any time, though they're not allowed to block one another to prevent passing. The winner is the skater who crosses the finish line first without committing a foul against any of the other skaters. Watching the 1994 Olympics, Ohno loved the fast pace of speedskating, as well as its sudden crashes, dramatic passes, and other exciting qualities. A short time later, he announced to his father that he intended to devote his athletic efforts toward mastering the sport. Within a matter of months, he was one of the finest short track skaters in the entire United States.

Less than a year after trying short track skating for the first time, Ohno was participating in speedskating events all across the United States and Canada. At age 13, he stunned the North American skating community by winning the U.S. National Long Track Championship, the prestigious Quebec Cup, and the U.S. National Short Track Championship in his age group (ages 13 and 14). He then capped his amazing year by claiming the North American Short Track Championship for 13- and 14-year-olds with victories in the 500 and 1,000 meter competitions and second and third place finishes in two other distance events.

These achievements placed Ohno squarely in the spotlight of America's competitive skating community. "For a skater his age, he's doing quite well," confirmed an assistant coach on the U.S. national speedskating team. But the coach added that Ohno was still looking at years of additional training if he hoped to make his mark on the sport as an adult. "One of the things you try to keep in mind when you see a juvenile is that the transition from being very good to world class is often one that very few people can make," the coach explained. "From what I can see, he will continue to develop . . . but if he wants to make an international impact he will need specialized training."

Skating Career Nearly Derailed by Defiant Behavior

During his early teens, Ohno's tremendous skating abilities became over-shadowed by rebellious and self-destructive behavior. He had always been high-spirited, but during this time his restless nature—and the large blocks of time that he spent without any adult supervision—led him to become involved with a crowd of older boys, some of whom were gang members. These new friends proved to be a nearly disastrous influence on Ohno. Eager to fit in, he went along with their schemes to skip school and vandalize school property. He also partied long into the night with them, letting his skating and school obligations fall by the wayside.

Ohno's father tried to rein him in, reminding him that he harbored dreams of competing in the Olympics one day. He even threatened to send Apolo to military school if he didn't shape up. But by age 14, Ohno was openly rebelling against his father and other authority figures. "If my dad said yes, I said no," he admitted. "That's the way it was for years. . . . There were times I'd go spend the night at a friend's house, and I wouldn't come home until like three days later."

Despite the deep strain in their relationship, Yuki Ohno continued to drive his son to skating meets all over North America. At one of these events, Apolo's father met with a skating coach on the U.S. Olympic Team and urged him to admit his 14-year-old son into the U.S. Olympic Training Center in Lake Placid, New York. Yuki Ohno knew that the minimum age for acceptance at the center was 15. But he felt that he was losing control of his son, and he hoped that the coaching staff's emphasis on discipline and supervision would help Apolo regain his focus on skating. Finally, Yuki Ohno knew that if his son was training in New York, he would no longer be under the influence of his troublesome friends.

"My dad was pretty frustrated with me," acknowledged Ohno. "But he had a schedule and no matter what he had to do, he was going to make me stick to it. He'd seen many parents who let their kids make life choices even though they had no understanding of life at that age. When it came to big decisions, my dad refused to give in. He didn't want me to look back on missed opportunities with regret and ask, 'Why didn't you stop me? Why'd you let me get away with this or that?' He firmly believed that if he let his child decide his own life path, it would lead to disaster."

"My dad was pretty frustrated with me. But he had a schedule and no matter what he had to do, he was going to make me stick to it. He'd seen many parents who let their kids make life choices even though they had no understanding of life at that age. When it came to big decisions, my dad refused to give in. He didn't want me to look back on missed opportunities with regret and ask, 'Why didn't you stop me? Why'd you let me get away with this or that?' He firmly believed that if he let his child decide his own life path, it would lead to disaster."

Moving to a Training Center

Eager to develop Apolo's raw skating talent, U.S. skating coach Patrick Wentland convinced U.S. Olympic Committee (USOC) officials to waive the minimum age requirement and admit Ohno into the training program at Lake Placid. But as it turned out, the young skater hated the idea of leaving Seattle for New York. When his father dropped him off at the Seattle airport in June 1996 for his flight to Lake Placid, Ohno did not board the plane. Instead, he fled to a friend's house and refused to come home for a week. His father finally convinced him to give the training program a try, but he was so worried about his son's behavior that he personally accompanied Apolo on the flight to New York.

On his own in Lake Placid at age 14, Ohno spent his first few days at the training center in a sullen funk. "I was so young," he recalled. "Totally rebellious against anything my dad or anybody in authority said. I hated the first month in Lake Placid. Moving from Seattle to New York is such a big change. Especially Lake Placid. It's just such a small town. I had never been in that kind of environment. I just felt kind of caged."

During his first weeks at Lake Placid, Ohno showed little interest in improving his skills as a skater. He did not show the same dedication toward training as the other athletes, and he often interrupted his conditioning runs with visits to the local pizza parlor. Not surprisingly, his poor dietary habits and indifference to training took their toll. One day, the coaches measured the body fat of all the skaters at Lake Placid. Ohno learned that he had a far higher percentage of body fat than any other athlete. Humiliated by this news, he decided to change his ways. "He came up to me and said, 'I don't want to be the fattest, I don't want to be the slowest, I want to be the best,'" remembered Wentland. "He totally changed. Every workout from then on, he had to win. I'd never seen that kind of turnaround so fast. Even now, at this level, if he decides one day that he's not feeling right, he won't skate well. But if he knows that he can win, I don't care if all the other skaters are having the best day of their lives, he'll beat them."

EDUCATION

Ohno attended elementary school in Washington in the Federal Way public school system. As a youngster he earned very good grades, and he spent some time in the honors program at Saghalie Junior High School. He eventually dropped out of the honors program, though, after his delinquent friends made fun of him.

Ohno started high school in Federal Way, but training obligations made it difficult for him to continue with a traditional education. He eventually earned his high school diploma by taking classes over the Internet. Ohno intended to go to college in 2001, but his intensive Olympic training regimen convinced him to delay enrollment. "I do, however, plan to go to college," he declared prior to the 2002 Games. "It is something that is very important to me. It's just so hard with my busy, unpredictable schedule right now with respect to training and competing."

CAREER HIGHLIGHTS

Ohno's time at Lake Placid during the summer of 1996 marked the beginning of his rise to international prominence. Determined to correct the nonchalant attitude that he had shown during his first weeks at the training center, he attacked his exercise and training program with a new dedication. His hard work paid off a year later, when he won the U.S. National Speedskating Championship at age 15, beating skaters that were 10 years older than him.

The speed of Ohno's ascent to the top ranking stunned even him. "Number one," he later wrote. "In less than a year I made it to the top of short track, and was ranked number one on the U.S. senior team. Nobody had ever excelled in the sport that quickly. There are steps to take and most long and short track skaters have been training since they were three years old. They've had plenty of ice time and come from strong skating clubs. They understand training, equipment management, and how to travel throughout the world. What's more, they've known each other for years. After less than a year on the junior team, I was not part of the inner circle, and even after the senior trials were over, the then-president of the speedskating association didn't come over to meet me or shake my hand."

> *"[Ohno] came up to me and said, 'I don't want to be the fattest, I don't want to be the slowest, I want to be the best,'" remembered U.S. skating coach Patrick Wentland. "He totally changed. Every workout from then on, he had to win. I'd never seen that kind of turnaround so fast. Even now, at this level, if he decides one day that he's not feeling right, he won't skate well. But if he knows that he can win, I don't care if all the other skaters are having the best day of their lives, he'll beat them."*

Struggling to Succeed

But Ohno still showed streaks of immaturity. Following his championship, he relocated to the Olympic Training Center in Colorado Springs, Colorado. There, he struggled to settle on a training and nutrition program that suited him. Then, when he returned to Seattle in the spring of 1997, he quickly slipped into his old self-destructive patterns of behavior. He let his training slide once again, and instead spent much of his time drinking and smoking with his friends. "I lost sight of my goals," he later admitted. "Drained after months of competitions and

A close-up of the crash in the 1,000-meter race at the 2002 Olympics: Ahn Hyun-soo (left) of South Korea, Mathieu Turcotte (center) of Canada, and Ohno (left).

the pressures of living on my own and taking care of every aspect of my sport, I didn't want to train anymore. I missed my friends; I needed a break; I wanted to take the summer off."

In August 1997, at age 16, Ohno traveled to a training camp in Chamonix, France, with the other American skaters. "I was in bad shape," he recalled. "[My coach] had told me to bike while home and put in lots of miles and I hadn't. Nor had I lifted weights, skated, stretched a muscle, or watched my diet—a bad combination of not working out, junk food, and puberty. . . . I couldn't beat anybody up at the camp—I got smoked on everything. My lungs burned on the bike rides through the hillsides of France, my legs burned during practices, my weights were lower than the other skaters and when we ran, I was in the back of the pack." At the conclusion of the camp, Ohno's coaches assured him that he still had time to get in shape for the January 1998 Olympic Trials. But when he returned home he "didn't train at all. There was a mountain in front of me, but I just sat down, ate a fat cheeseburger, and didn't even try to climb it."

In January 1998 Ohno went to the U.S. speedskating trials, which would determine who would represent America at the 1998 Winter Olympics in Nagano, Japan. Experts who were unaware of Ohno's summertime difficulties believed that he would easily make the team. In fact, many people felt that he was a legitimate contender for a medal at the Nagano games.

But as Ohno later admitted, "I had no expectations at all. I wasn't ready for the Olympic trials at all. I was overweight, I hadn't been training, my technique was horrible. Mentally, I didn't even care."

As it turned out, Ohno not only failed to make the Olympic team, but he turned in the worst performance of the 16 skaters who competed in the trials. "It was devastating for him," recalled Yuki Ohno. "It's a thing that can end an athlete's career, right there. Or take two to three years to recover from."

Changing His Attitude

In the days following the Olympic trials, Ohno wandered around in a daze. "I felt like I let a lot of people down," he said. "I was destroyed. I was crushed." Ohno's father knew that Apolo needed to have some time to himself, so he arranged for his troubled son to spend a week at a remote cabin on the Washington coast. He dropped Ohno off at the cabin and departed, leaving the talented but confused teenager to decide what he wanted to do with his life.

At first, Ohno found the cabin's isolated location to be a little unsettling. "There was no TV, no telephone, nothing," he remembered. "There was the ocean, and there was the sand, trees. That's it." But the week of seclusion helped him immensely. As he passed the days wandering along the beach or running through the woods, he realized that he was wasting his talent. By the time he returned home,

After Ohno failed to make the 1998 Olympic team, he realized that "Everything had changed. My career had both ended and begun anew. . . . And I also understood for the first time in my life that I couldn't accomplish everything alone. I'd known that it took coaches to help, but now I really got that it takes a team to transform someone with raw talent into a champion — coaches, sports trainers, friends, and fans. Most of all it takes the consistency of always having someone in your corner. After that trip to the cottage my father became my true partner in short track."

he had rededicated himself to conditioning, training, and improving his mental attitude. "Everything had changed. My career had both ended and begun anew. I recognized that I was talented and had a gift. I realized that I loved my sport. And I also understood for the first time in my life that I couldn't accomplish everything alone. I'd known that it took coaches to help, but now I really got that it takes a team to transform someone with raw talent into a champion—coaches, sports trainers, friends, and fans. Most of all it takes the consistency of always having someone in your corner. After that trip to the cottage my father became my true partner in short track."

—————— " ——————

Ohno expressed heartfelt appreciation for his dad's efforts as a single parent and for his unwavering support. "It's definitely a close-knit relationship between my father and me. He raised me my whole life, and I went through a lot with my dad. He's been a big influence in my life in skating and in my decisions in life. I didn't ever really know that I was supposed to have a mom. My dad's been in my career for as long as I've been skating . . . . He's sacrificed just about as much as I have."

—————— " ——————

In 1998 and 1999 Ohno dramatically improved his conditioning and technique, and he gradually proved that he was once again a force to be reckoned with. In a December 1999 competition in Chang Chun, China, he became the youngest American skater ever to win a World Cup event, the most prestigious competitions—other than the Olympics—in the sport. Afterward, Ohno freely admitted that the victory was his greatest accomplishment to that point in his career. He followed this triumph with a string of impressive performances, and by the end of the 1999 season he was ranked seventh in the World Cup standings.

Breaking Out

Ohno opened the 2000-2001 season in October 2000 by securing his second title in World Cup competition. He remained steady for the remainder of the campaign, and by the close of the year he was the top ranked short track speedskater in the entire world. His triumphs included gold medals in three different events (1,500 meters, 1,000 meters, and 500 meters) at the World Cup Short Track Speedskating Championships, and recognition as the World Cup circuit's Short Track Speedskating Overall Champion for the year.

Ohno describes the 2000-2001 season as his "breakout" year, explaining that he "was dominating like no other skater." But early in 2001 a back injury threatened to derail his career. "With only seven months before the 2002 Olympic Trials, I needed three months of intensive rehabilitation to be able to perform at 80 percent of my abilities. I couldn't skate or train

Ohno (left) skates with Guo Wei (center) of China and Nicky Gooch (right) during the semifinals of the men's 1,500-meter speedskating competition at the 2002 Olympics.

and I saw my Olympic dreams sliding away along with my fitness with each day, week, and month. The mental toll of knowing that my predicted performance level after rehabilitation would still only be 80 percent was brutal."

During this period of his life, Ohno's relationship with his father became even closer. He expressed heartfelt appreciation for his dad's efforts as a single parent and for his unwavering support for Ohno's athletic aspirations. "It's definitely a close-knit relationship between my father and me," he stated. "He raised me my whole life, and I went through a lot with my dad. He's been a big influence in my life in skating and in my decisions in life. I didn't ever really know that I was supposed to have a mom. My dad's been in my career for as long as I've been skating. . . . He's sacrificed just about as much as I have."

Preparing for the Olympics

The tragic terrorist attacks of September 11, 2001, had a major impact on the 2001-2002 World Cup season. Training schedules and competitions were changed, and some athletes—like Ohno—ended up competing in only one or two events. At the same time, Ohno remained engaged in a grim struggle to conquer his back injury and salvage his dream of Olympic competition. "Four months before the Games I started to train hard again," he recalled. "Agonizing muscle spasms ripped through my back and forced me off the ice at first, but with each day I improved. When I made it to the Olympic Trials, I was thrilled by how far I had come."

At the U.S. Olympic trials in December 2001, the young skating sensation served notice that he was at the top of his game when he set a world record in the 1,500 meters with a time of 2:13:728. In fact, he qualified to compete in all four speedskating events — the 500-, 1,000-, and 1,500-meter individual events and the 5,000-meter relay. "When I qualified to skate in each individual event in the Games, plus the relay, I felt like I'd reached the top of the mountain," he recalled. "I had given 110 percent to get there and was euphoric."

> "When I qualified to skate in each individual event in the [Olympic] Games, plus the relay, I felt like I'd reached the top of the mountain. I had given 110 percent to get there and was euphoric."

But as the trials progressed, he also became embroiled in an ugly controversy. He and teammate Rusty Smith were accused of purposely posting poor performances in the 1,000-meter finals so that one of Ohno's friends would make the squad. But the elevation of this friend to the Olympic squad came at the expense of another American skater, Tom O'Hare, who was subsequently left off the team. A few weeks after the Olympic trials, O'Hare files charges against Ohno, claiming that he cheated to help his friend.

The U.S. Olympic Committee hired an independent judge, called an arbitrator, to hear the case. As the hearing progressed, some witnesses offered damaging testimony. Three athletes claimed that they overheard Ohno plotting to cheat. The head referee during the disputed race also testified that Ohno's performance during the competition was very suspicious. But other officials and skaters supported his claim that he had an average skating performance because he was concerned about getting an injury that might carry over to the Olympics.

When the hearing was over, the independent arbitrator cleared Ohno of all charges, saying that there was not enough evidence of wrongdoing. A short time later, O'Hare dropped the issue. For his part, Ohno stated that he was "very pleased with the outcome. I knew the truth would come out.

Ohno skates close on the heels of Kim Dong-sung of South Korea during the men's 1500-meter speedskating finals at the 2002 Olympics. Kim crossed the finish line first but was disqualified, giving the gold medal to Ohno.

I was concerned because I was losing training time and losing focus, but I'm definitely getting back on track."

A Media Sensation

As the 2002 Winter Olympics approached, Ohno became the focus of a great deal of media attention. After all, he was a leading medal candidate in four different Olympic events — the 500-, 1,000-, and 1,500-meter individual events and the 5,000-meter relay. In addition, he had acquired a sort of rock star mystique because of his unusual name, his long mane of hair, his "soul patch" — a stripe of facial hair that extended from his lower lip to his chin — and his casual attitude. This combination proved irresistible to the media, and in the weeks leading up to the Olympics Ohno gave countless interviews for television, newspapers, magazines, and the Internet. He even appeared on the cover of *Sports Illustrated*.

Ohno admitted that all the attention increased the pressure on him to perform well. But he added that "I'm going to do my thing and just pretty much try to perform the best I can regardless of what's happening around me. It's short-track — anything can happen. If I make one mistake, if I'm a hundredth of a second too late in a pass, then the race is over. So you definitely have got to have the golden horseshoe if you're going to win four [gold medals]."

Despite all the uncertainties, however, Ohno also expressed confidence that he would make an impact in the speedskating events. "Skating as well as I am—that's special," he said. "To be able to come out of that mess as I did is special. To be able to improve my relations with my dad is special. I'm happy with the way my life's going, the way I'm growing up as a person. Skating has changed me. I've had a lot of chances, and this is my time to shine."

The 2002 Olympics

After Ohno arrived in Salt Lake City, Utah, for the 2002 Winter Olympic Games, his first event was the 1,000-meter race. When he arrived at the stadium, he was stunned to find more than 15,000 fans hoarsely screaming for Ohno. Many people in the crowd were even sporting fake soul patches on their chins to show support for the young man from Seattle. "I can't even describe how I felt [to see the crowd]," he later said. "My heart rate was definitely pumped up. I worked hard just to stay relaxed."

In the finals of the 1,000 meters, Ohno cruised to the front and kept the lead. But in the final turn, he and skater Li Jiajun of China tangled up and took two other racers out in a big crash. The last place skater, Australian Steven Bradbury, dashed through the fallen racers to claim the gold medal. Ohno, meanwhile, crawled across the finish line to claim second place, even though he had suffered a cut on his thigh that eventually required six stitches to close.

The race's conclusion sparked roars of boos from the crowd, which had packed the stadium to see Ohno win gold. But Susan Ellis, the head coach of the U.S. short track squad, shrugged off the crowd's reaction. "If you don't want to occasionally crash into the boards and lose, then you shouldn't do short track," she said. "Just like if you don't want to maybe fall down real hard and break a leg, you don't do downhill skiing. Those are the risks."

Ohno, meanwhile, showed great sportsmanship in his post-race actions and comments. He expressed delight at winning the silver medal and offered hearty congratulations to Bradbury. After all, he knew that the Australian skater had endured years of injury—including a broken neck in 2000 and a 1994 crash in which he cut his leg so badly on a skate that he nearly died, losing four of the six liters of blood in his body—in order to fulfill his dream of competing in the Olympics.

Ohno during the playing of the national anthem after being awarded the gold medal in the 1500-meter men's speed skating event at the 2002 Olympics.

Winning the Gold Medal

Ohno's next event was the 1,500 meters. He easily advanced to the medal round, where he once again found himself in a tight battle for gold. As the skaters entered the final lap, Ohno was in second place, right behind Kim Dong-sung of South Korea. Ohno tried to slip past Dong-sung, only to have the frontrunner block his route. A moment later, Dong-sung crossed the finish line first for an apparent gold medal, but he was later disqualified for his blocking action against Ohno. This disqualification gave Ohno his first Olympic gold medal.

South Korean officials and fans were furious about the disqualification. Some representatives of the South Korean team threatened to boycott (refuse to participate in) the rest of the Olympics, and fans sent thousands of angry e-mails to Ohno. But the young American refused to let the South Korean reaction spoil his moment of glory. "I just feel so good," he said. "I come here, perform my best, and get a gold medal. There's nothing better than that."

Ohno's final two events ended in disappointment. In the 500-meter race, he was disqualified in a semifinal round when he accidentally knocked a Japanese skater to the ice. This made him ineligible to compete in the final

117

round, when medal winners would be determined. Team USA then failed to medal in the 5,000-meter relay when one of Ohno's teammates fell during the race. The team could only manage a fourth-place finish.

The outcomes of these races left Ohno without the four Olympic medals that some people had predicted. But Ohno insisted that his Olympic experience had been fantastic. "I'm not disappointed at all, I've got a silver and a gold," he said. "My quest, my journey wasn't about winning four golds. It's about coming to the Olympics, enjoying the experience and doing my best, regardless of the medal outcome."

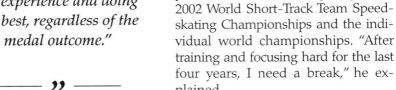

Ohno says that his Olympic experience was fantastic. "I'm not disappointed at all, I've got a silver and a gold. My quest, my journey wasn't about winning four golds. It's about coming to the Olympics, enjoying the experience and doing my best, regardless of the medal outcome."

When the Olympics ended, Ohno returned home to Seattle, where he received a huge welcome. The city declared March 15, 2002, as "Apolo Ohno Day" and held a variety of events in the young skater's honor. Ohno then set out on a media tour that took him all across the country. He appeared on "The Tonight Show with Jay Leno," "The Conan O'Brien Show," and a host of other nationally televised programs. These activities prevented him from competing in the 2002 World Short-Track Team Speedskating Championships and the individual world championships. "After training and focusing hard for the last four years, I need a break," he explained.

But Ohno has made it clear that he fully intends to make a splash at the 2006 Winter Olympics. "I'll be training day in and day out *not* for a handful of gold medals, but to be the best ever—the best short track skater of all time. Skating is what I want to do for the next four years. I love to compete against the elite of my sport and to work on my technique every single day, *because* it's so hard."

HOBBIES AND OTHER INTERESTS

Ohno enjoys listening to rap and rhythm and blues music, dancing, and playing basketball and badminton. He also likes summertime activities like boating and jetskiing. After his days as a competitive skater are over, he has expressed interest in becoming a coach, a computer programmer, or a motivational speaker for junior high school kids. "That's really the age bracket where children can start to go down the wrong path, but it's still early enough that they can change their lives," Ohno explained. "I want to tell kids what I did when I was younger. It's important for them to understand that I think it's cool to be smart and in an honors program, and that I believe it's vitally important to finish high school and continue education at a higher level."

HOME AND FAMILY

Ohno, who remains unmarried, lives in Colorado Springs, Colorado.

WRITINGS

Ohno, Apolo Anton, and Nancy Ann Richardson. *A Journey: The Autobiography of Apolo Anton Ohno,* 2002

HONORS AND AWARDS

U.S. National Speedskating Champion: 1997, 1999, 2001, 2002
World Short Track Speedskating Championships: 1999, Silver Medal
Junior World Short Track Speedskating Championships: 1999, First Place
U.S. Junior Short Track Overall Champion: 2000
World Cup Short Track Speedskating Championships: 2001, Gold Medal
    (1,500 meters), Gold Medal (1,000 meters), Gold Medal (500 meters)
World Cup Short Track Speedskating Overall Champion: 2001
Olympic Short Track Speedskating: 2002, Gold Medal (1,500 meters),
    Silver Medal (1,000 meters)
Pan-Pacific Excellence Award: 2002

FURTHER READING

Books

Lang, Thomas. *Apolo Anton Ohno: Going for the Gold,* 2002 (juvenile)
Layden, Joe. *All About Apolo!* 2002 (juvenile)
Ohno, Apolo Anton, and Nancy Ann Richardson. *A Journey: The Autobiography of Apolo Anton Ohno,* 2002

Periodicals

Boys' Life, Jan. 1999, p.12
Denver Post, Jan. 25, 2002, p.A1; Feb. 25, 2002, p.D4
Detroit Free Press, Feb. 9, 2002, Section Sports, p.3

Houston Chronicle, Feb. 15, 2002, p.3
Kansas City (Kans.) Star, Dec. 14, 2001, p.D4
New York Times Upfront, Feb. 11, 2002, p.25
People, May 13, 2002, p.99
Rolling Stone, Apr. 11, 2002, p.111
San Francisco Chronicle, Feb. 3, 2002, p.B9
Seattle Post-Intelligencer, Mar. 25, 1997, p.D1; Mar. 16, 2002, p.A1
Seattle Times, Mar. 15, 1996, p.C1; Apr. 9, 1996, p.C5; Dec. 27, 1998, p.D1;
    Oct. 23, 2000, p.D14; Mar. 28, 2002, p.D2; June 14, 2002, p.G1
Sports Illustrated, Feb. 4, 2002, p.122; Feb. 25, 2002, p.46
Sports Illustrated for Kids, Feb. 1, 2002, p.56; May 1, 2002, p.6
St. Louis Post-Dispatch, Feb. 14, 2002, p.D1
Teen People, Feb. 2002, p.82; Nov. 2002, p.124
Time, Feb. 11, 2002, p.52
USA Today, Nov. 1, 2001, p.C15
Washington Post, December 22, 2001, p.D1

Online Articles

http://www.usaweekend.com/02_issues/020407/020407whosnews_
    ohno.html
    (*USA Weekend.com,* "Q and A: Apolo Anton Ohno," April 7, 2002)
http://teacher.scholastic.com/newszone/specialreports/olympics/athletes
    (*Scholastic,* "Apolo Ohno," undated)

Online Databases

Biography Resource Center Online, 2002

ADDRESS

Apolo Ohno
U.S. Speedskating
Utah Olympic Oval
5662 South 4800 West
Kearns, UT 84118

WORLD WIDE WEB SITES

http://www.olympic-usa.org
http://www.usspeedskating.org
http://www.cyberscoreboard.com/profile.php?Athlete=6133

Sylke Otto 1969-

German Luge Athlete
Winner of the Gold Medal in the Women's Single
Luge Event at the 2002 Winter Olympics

BIRTH

Sylke Otto was born on July 7, 1969, in Karl-Marx Stadt, East
Germany. At the time of Otto's birth, the city in which she
was born was part of Communist-controlled East Germany
(Germany had split into two distinct countries after its defeat
in World War II in 1945). In 1990, however, East Germany and
West Germany became one country again under a process

called reunification. After the two regions were reunited under a single democratically elected government, the name of Otto's hometown was changed back to Chemnitz, its original name before Communist control.

YOUTH AND EDUCATION

Otto enjoyed an active and athletic childhood in Chemnitz. Like many other Germans, she was especially fond of winter sports like skiing, skating, and luge. In luge (also known as toboggan) competitions, participants race down an icy downhill course while lying on a sled. Since participants are lying on their backs, with their feet pointed downhill, they can only use their legs and shoulders to guide the sled, which can reach very high speeds. As a result, luge is regarded as one of the more dangerous sports in the world.

By her early teens, Otto showed so much athletic promise that she attracted the attention of the East German government. Like many other Communist countries at that time, East Germany sponsored the training of its top athletes in order to build teams capable of dominating international competition. In addition, the East German government exercised a great deal of control over the personal lives of its citizens. Government authorities used their power to place Otto in an elite athletic training school, and from that time forward she spent hours every day practicing for luge competitions.

Otto participated in her first luge events in 1983, and for the rest of the decade she continued to train under the expert eyes of East Germany's top instructors. Her long years of hard work paid off when she was named a member of East Germany's national luge team in the late 1980s. Around this same period, she entered the East German army. For Otto and most other East German elite athletes of the era, military service was a requirement, not an option. But authorities arranged her schedule so that she could continue to represent her country in international competitions.

CAREER HIGHLIGHTS

When East and West Germany reunited in 1990, their Olympic programs also merged. This turn of events made the competition for berths on the German national team even more intense. But Otto responded to the challenge. Showing great talent and determination, she secured a spot on the German team for the 1992 Winter Olympic Games to be held in Albertville, France. Up to 1992, both the Winter and the Summer Olympic Games took place in the same year, every four years. After that, the two sets of games were staggered, with the Winter Games in 1994 (and every four years thereafter) and the Summer Games in 1996 (and every four years thereafter).

At the 1992 Winter Olympics, Otto posted a respectable 13th-place finish in the women's single luge event in the Games. But in 1994 she failed to secure a spot on the German national team for the Winter Olympics held in Lillehammer, Norway. Despite this disappointment, she emerged as a force to be reckoned with in international luge events during the 1994-1995 season. She raced well in event after event on the World Cup circuit, which is the premier competition for luge competitors. By the end of the season, she had earned the Overall World Cup Championship for the 1994-1995 season, her first time winning this major award. Since the mid-1990s, Otto has consistently finished among the top contenders in both single and team events in the World Luge Championships as well as the World Cup Championships.

One of Otto's fans is Heinze-Michael Kirsten, the mayor of Oberwiesenthal, a winter sports training center in Germany where she spends lots of time. "She is very kind and not so high on herself," explained Kirsten. "We like the whole German team. . . . But Sylke is our favorite. She always has a lot of fun with us."

Part of the German Luge Machine

Otto's championship established her as an important part of Germany's luge squad, which was gaining a reputation as one of the best in the world. In 1997 she helped Germany's women's luge team secure a team silver medal in the World Luge Championships, and in 1999 she earned bronze medals in both the single and team events in the World Luge Championships. In the meantime, Otto continued to accumulate individual honors. In addition to winning numerous individual World Cup events, she finished second in the World Cup Overall standings for the 1998-1999 season.

But when it came to the Olympics, Otto's otherwise stellar career received another blow in 1998. She once again failed to qualify for the German Olympic team in the women's single luge event. She finished fourth in qualifying, and each country is only allowed to send three athletes for the event. As she watched her teammates compete at the 1998 Winter Olympics in Nagano, Japan, she was delighted that fellow Germans Silke Kraushaar and Barbara Niedernhuber were able to claim the

*Otto celebrates her victory in a women's luge event in Austria
for the 1998 World Cup.*

gold and silver medals in the women's single luge competition. But as Otto watched them accept their medals, she could not help but wonder if she would ever again have an opportunity to perform on the Olympic stage.

In 2000, Otto continued to perform at a rare level of excellence. She clinched the Overall World Cup Championship for the 1999-2000 season, for the second time in her career. Then at the 2000 World Luge Championships in St. Moritz, Switzerland, she shook off an ugly crash at the very end of her first run to win the gold medal in the women's single luge event; she also won a silver medal in the team competition. She capped her great season with a gold medal finish at the 2000 Goodwill Games in Lake Placid, New York. Otto continued to remain a major force in the world of luge in 2001. Major triumphs included the gold medal in the single event at the European Luge Championship; the the silver medal in the team competition and the gold medal in the single event at the World Luge Championship; and a second-place finish for 2000-2001 in the overall standings for the World Cup Championship.

These triumphs secured Otto's place as one of Germany's most popular athletes. In Germany, skiers, lugers, and other athletes who compete in winter sports are almost as popular as professional football and basketball players in the United States. Otto even has a small but devoted fan club that cheers her on at events all around Europe. One member of the fan club is Heinze-Michael Kirsten, the mayor of Oberwiesenthal, a winter sports training center in Germany where Otto spends lots of time. "She is very kind and not so high on herself," explained Kirsten. "We like the whole German team. . . . But Sylke is our favorite. She always has a lot of fun with us."

As the 2002 Olympics approached, Otto expressed confidence that she would do well. "I am very pleased with my training runs. I am feeling very confident. I am not making any big mistakes but I am working on lots of little ones."

In January 2002 Otto successfully defended her European Luge Championship title with a series of beautiful runs. "It's good Otto pulled a couple of runs like that out of her hat," said Kraushaar, who remained both her teammate and her primary competition for women's single luge supremacy. "Now I know I have to work on my sled before the Olympics." A week later Otto posted her worst finish of the 2001-2002 World Cup season in a race in Latvia. She finished fourth, while Kraushaar won the race. Still, Otto went on to finish second in the Overall World Cup Championship for the season. Then in February 2002, Otto took the gold medal at the World Luge Championship, clinching her third consecutive single luge title.

Otto competes during the women's singles luge event at the 2002 Olympics.

A Triumphant Return to the Olympics

Otto made her second appearance as an Olympian at the 2002 Winter Games in Salt Lake City, Utah. "It is so good to be here," she declared. Otto admitted that her failure to make the Olympic team in 1994 and 1998 — especially after her promising Olympic performance in 1992 — had tested her resolve. "Those ten years were tough and several times I wanted to quit," she admitted. "In 1998 I just missed the team and I said to myself, 'I will be there in 2002.'"

As the women's single luge competition approached, Otto expressed confidence that she would do well. "I am very pleased with my training runs. I am feeling very confident. I am not making any big mistakes but I am working on lots of little ones." But she also recognized that her teammates Silke Kraushaar and Barbara Niedernhuber would be difficult to beat. Indeed, Kraushaar and Niedernhuber had earned the gold and silver medals respectively in the women's single luge competition at the 1998 Olympics. In addition, Kraushaar and Otto had combined to win 29 of the last 35 World Cup events leading up to the 2002 Games. "Everybody on our team wants to be the best," said Otto. "That's the reason why we have such a strong team. There's always competition between us."

The women's single luge event at Salt Lake City was held on February 12 and 13, 2002. Each day, each competitor made two runs down the twisting, 1,140-meter (1,242-yard) course. The gold medal for the event goes to the luger that posts the best total or aggregate time after all four runs are added together.

Otto seized the lead after the first day of the two-day competition. She performed flawlessly, racing down the icy course as if she had been shot out of a cannon. Afterwards, she expressed satisfaction with her effort. But she also noted that her teammates were right on her heels, ready to pounce on any mistake.

On her first run of February 13, however, Otto served notice that she intended to claim the gold medal for herself. She clocked a new course record of 42.940 seconds that enabled her to open up a big lead over Kraushaar and the other athletes in the competition. Otto then completed a solid fourth run, and as she crossed the finish line she pumped her arms in triumph and happiness. She knew that after more than a decade of frustration and disappointment, she had finally fulfilled her dream of winning an Olympic gold medal. "I don't know what to say," she exclaimed afterward. "I can't believe it. Finally, I've made it and it was a long way to go for this medal. I'm totally happy."

In the meantime, Kraushaar and Niedernhuber claimed second and third place in the competition, giving the German team a clean sweep of the medals in the event. This sweep helped the German team set a new Winter Olympics record for total medals won with 35, including 12 gold medals. "Some people say that it's boring, that it's always us winning," admitted Otto. "But if we don't win what will people say then?"

HOME AND FAMILY

Sylke Otto lives in Zirndorf, Germany. Her boyfriend is Ronald Grund, who helped organize the Sylke Otto fan club.

HOBBIES AND OTHER INTERESTS

Otto enjoys gardening and cooking in her free time.

HONORS AND AWARDS

European Luge Championships (team competition): 1990, Gold Medal; 1992, Silver Medal; 2000, Gold Medal
European Luge Championships (singles): 1992, Silver Medal; 2000, Gold Medal; 2001, Gold Medal; 2002, Gold Medal
World Cup Championship, Overall: 1994-1995, First Place; 1998-1999, Second Place; 1999-2000, First Place; 2000-2001, Second Place; 2001-2002, Second Place

World Luge Championships (team competition): 1997, Silver Medal; 1999,
    Bronze Medal; 2000, Silver Medal; 2001, Silver Medal
World Luge Championships (singles): 1999, Bronze Medal; 2000, Gold
    Medal; 2001, Gold Medal; 2002, Gold Medal
Goodwill Games (women's singles): 2000, Gold Medal
Olympic Luge (women's singles): 2002, Gold Medal

FURTHER READING

Books

Wallachinsky, David. *The Complete Book of the Winter Olympics: Salt Lake
    City 2002,* 2001

Periodicals

Boston Globe, Feb. 14, 2002, p.C4
Calgary (Alb.) Herald, Feb. 24, 2001, p.D5
Calgary (Alb.) Sun, Feb. 24, 2001, p.F1; Feb. 25, 2001, p.S9
Denver Rocky Mountain News, Feb. 13, 2002, p.S10; Feb. 14, 2002, p.S10
Houston Chronicle, Feb. 13, 2002, p.3
Los Angeles Times, Feb. 14, 2002, p.U5
Salt Lake Tribune, Feb. 19, 2000, p.C1; Feb. 14, 2002, p.O11
Washington Post, Feb. 14, 2002, p.D11

Online Articles

http://www.bbc.co.uk/winterolympics2002/low/english/luge_and_skeleton/
    (*BBC News*, "Otto Leads German Clean Sweep,"Feb. 14, 2002)

ADDRESS

Sylke Otto
National Olympic Committee of Germany
Postfach 71 02 63
DE - 60492 Frankfurt-am-Main
Germany

WORLD WIDE WEB SITES

http://www.fil-luge.org
http://www.sylkeotto.de (German language)

BRIEF ENTRY

Ryne Sanborn 1989-

American Student
"Child of Light" Skater in the Opening and Closing
Ceremonies of the 2002 Winter Olympics

EARLY YEARS

Ryne (pronounced RINE) Sanborn was born on February 3,
1989. His parents, Jeff and Florence Sanborn, named him after
Ryne Sandberg, the star second baseman of the Chicago Cubs.
Ryne has a younger sister, Danielle.

Sanborn has grown up in West Valley City, a suburb of Salt Lake City, Utah. He enjoys participating in all kinds of sports, from baseball and soccer to skateboarding and snowboarding. His favorite sport is hockey, which he plays competitively in Salt Lake City's Wamaha League. "I just love to play hockey and skate," he says. Sanborn has also done some acting and modeling from an early age. He has appeared in catalogs for J.C. Penney and REI and in several television commercials. He has also had small roles on the TV series "Touched by an Angel" and in a couple of TV movies.

——— **"** ———

In the fall of 2001, Sanborn attended an ice skating audition for the Olympic opening ceremony. "I went with a bunch of my hockey buddies to an audition at a regular skating rink, and we skated around through some cones, over some cones. And I came for a callback and skated around a little bit, and they took me into a little room and said I was the main child."

———  ———

MAJOR ACCOMPLISHMENT

Preparing for the 2002 Winter Olympic Games

In the fall of 2001, organizers of the 2002 Winter Olympic Games—which were to be held in Salt Lake City—began holding auditions for cast members to appear in the opening and closing ceremonies. One of the auditions called for children who knew how to ice skate. Sanborn attended the audition with several members of his hockey team. "I went with a bunch of my hockey buddies to an audition at a regular skating rink, and we skated around through some cones, over some cones," he remembered. "And I came for a callback and skated around a little bit, and they took me into a little room and said I was the main child."

Olympic organizers explained that Sanborn would portray the "Child of Light" in the opening and closing ceremonies. The theme of the Salt Lake City Games was "Light the Fire Within." As the main character in the ceremonies, he would skate around a large ice rink on the floor of Rice-Eccles Stadium while carrying a lantern. As his father described it, "He would be representing humanity and the struggle to overcome adversity using the fire within each of us."

Sanborn prepared for his role by taking figure skating lessons once a week for several months. He recalled that his hockey friends "thought it was

Sanborn (center) performs as the "Child of Light" at the opening ceremony of the 2002 Winter Olympics.

kind of girly, but they thought it was really cool in the end when it was all done." He also had to let his hair grow long. Rehearsals for the ceremonies took up a great deal of time. Sanborn was forced to miss some of his seventh-grade classes at Valley Junior High, and he struggled to keep up with his homework. To make matters worse, he was not allowed to tell any of his friends, relatives, or teachers what he was doing. The content of the Olympic opening and closing ceremonies are always kept secret.

Performing in the Opening Ceremony

The opening ceremony for the Winter Olympics in Salt Lake City took place on the evening of February 8, 2002. The three-hour extravaganza — which featured 3,500 cast members and cost an estimated $35 million — was watched in the stadium by 60,000 spectators. In addition, an estimated three billion people around the world watched it on television.

One segment of the opening ceremony honored Utah's Native American heritage. In fact, representatives of the five indigenous tribes of Utah (the Ute, Goshute, Shoshone, Paiute, and Navajo nations) were the first to greet the Olympic athletes as they entered the stadium. Another segment celebrated the pioneers who settled Utah and the American West. This part of the show featured covered wagons making their way through bears,

131

snakes, and bison that were created with special effects. The night also included a performance by the Dixie Chicks country-rock band and a duet by classical cellist Yo-Yo Ma and pop singer Sting.

Perhaps the most emotional moment of the opening ceremony came when New York City police officers and firefighters unfurled a tattered American flag that had been found in the rubble of the World Trade Center following the terrorist attacks of September 11, 2001. The flag was illuminated while the Mormon Tabernacle Choir sang the Star-Spangled Banner. Some people had criticized plans to display this flag, claiming that it was inappropriate to commemorate an American tragedy at an international sporting event. But Olympic organizers pointed out that citizens of 80 countries had died when the World Trade Center collapsed. By comparison, the athletes participating in the 2002 Winter Olympics represented 77 countries.

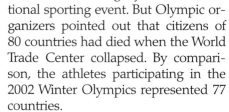

Sanborn portrayed the "Child of Light" in the opening and closing ceremonies, whose theme was "Light the Fire Within." As his father described it, "He would be representing humanity and the struggle to overcome adversity using the fire within each of us."

A group of famous people representing all seven of the world's continents carried the Olympic flag into the stadium. Then a series of American gold medalists from past Winter Games carried the Olympic torch into the stadium. These athletes included figure skaters Dorothy Hamill, Peggy Fleming, Dick Button, and Scott Hamilton; downhill skiers Phil Mahre, Bill Johnson, and Picabo Street; and speed skaters Dan Jansen and Bonnie Blair.

In addition, the ceremony included the 1980 U.S. Olympic hockey team, which defeated a powerful Russian team for the gold medal in a game known as the "Miracle on Ice" in the 1980 Winter Olympics in Lake Placid, New York. The hockey team members accepted the torch from the final bearers and lit the Olympic flame. President George W. Bush then gave a short speech and officially opened the Games.

Sanborn helped tie together the various elements of the opening ceremony. Dressed in a red jacket and hat, he skated around the stadium carrying a lantern. He made his way past several obstacles, including a spectacular storm generated with lights and special effects. Just as it seemed that he would be overcome by his struggles, he found the fire within himself. This fire spread to hundreds of other children on the stadium floor. Immediately

Sanborn as the "Child of Light" carries a lanter through a winter forest at the opening ceremony of the 2002 Winter Olympics.

afterward, the more than 2,500 Olympic athletes began marching into the stadium. Overall, the opening ceremony received a great deal of praise for being artistic and inspiring.

Sanborn performed flawlessly throughout the evening, although he admitted that he once "caught an edge" of his skate and came close to falling. His parents were far more worried about his performance than he was. "I was so nervous, sick to my stomach, but he was fine," his mother admitted. Sanborn claimed that his favorite part of the opening ceremony was meeting the stars of the 1980 U.S. hockey team. He also was inspired by the World Trade Center flag, since his grandfather had been a New York police officer.

Skating in the Closing Ceremony

Sanborn's friends, relatives, and classmates were shocked when they recognized him skating on television. Some people were angry that he had not told them about his role in the opening ceremony. But Sanborn explained that the Olympic organizers had sworn him to secrecy. He was allowed to tell people that he would also appear in the closing ceremony, though he was not allowed to say exactly what he would do.

During the three weeks between the opening and closing ceremonies, Sanborn acted as a sort of goodwill ambassador at the Games. He greeted athletes and fans, took part in promotional events, and assisted at medal ceremonies. He and the other "children of light" were supposed to represent the dreams inside everyone and inspire people to do their best and succeed.

The closing ceremony of the Salt Lake City Olympics took place on February 24. More lighthearted than the opening ceremony, it featured musical performances by Christina Aguilera, Bon Jovi, Gloria Estefan, Kiss, Harry Connick Jr., Willie Nelson, and *N Sync. Sanborn once again played the "Child of Light," skating a routine alongside former gold medal winners Katarina Witt and Scott Hamilton. Then he led a chorus of 780 Utah children singing "Happy Trails to You." The mayor of Salt Lake City handed over the Olympic flag to the mayor of Turin, Italy, the city that will host the 2006 Winter Games. Finally, the Olympic torch was extinguished to mark the end of the Games.

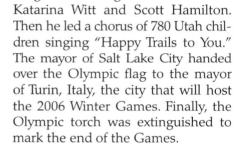

"It was the most extraordinary experience I've ever had and most likely will ever have," Sanborn stated. "It was totally awesome."

Sanborn received a great deal of attention following his roles in the Olympic opening and closing ceremonies. He was interviewed on "Today" and on several local TV stations. He auditioned for a part in a Disney movie and was contacted about appearing in Tommy Hilfiger ads. He also received a flood of notes and phone calls from girls asking him out. "It was the most extraordinary experience I've ever had and most likely will ever have," Sanborn stated. "It was totally awesome." The only negative part of the experience was that his grades dropped, and his father put his PlayStation off-limits until he got his schoolwork under control again. Still, he claims that the experience taught him to "go for what you want and be all you can be, because in the end it pays off."

FUTURE PLANS

Sanborn hopes to become a professional hockey player or an Olympic snowboarder someday. "When I turn 14, I'd like to work at Zumiez, the skateboarding store," he says.

HOBBIES AND OTHER INTERESTS

Sanborn enjoys participating in all sorts of sports. He plays baseball, soccer, and hockey, and he also likes in-line skating, snowboarding, and skateboarding. In his spare time, he practices the electric guitar.

FURTHER READING

Periodicals

New York Times, Feb. 9, 2002, p.A1
Salt Lake City Deseret News, Mar. 19, 2002, p.B1
Salt Lake Tribune, Feb. 8, 2002, p.C1; Feb. 9, 2002, p.O10
USA Today, Feb. 9, 2002, p.1
Washington Post, Feb. 10, 2002, p.D1

Online Articles

http://teacher.scholastic.com/newszone/specialreports/olympics/2002/
dailyreports.htm
(*Scholastic,* "America Says So Long to Winter Olympics," Feb. 25, 2002)
http://216.247.63.129/stories/olyryne.htm
(*Detroit Free Press,* "Yakking with a Child of Light," undated)

Other

Additional information for this profile was taken from an interview on "Today," broadcast Feb. 11, 2002, on NBC-TV.

ADDRESS

Ryne Sanborn
P.O. Box 702706
Salt Lake City, UT 84170

Jim Shea, Jr. 1968-

American Skeleton Athlete
Winner of the Gold Medal in Men's Skeleton at the
2002 Winter Olympics
First Third-Generation Winter Olympian

BIRTH

Jim Shea, Jr., was born on June 10, 1968, in Hartford, Connecticut. His father, Jim Shea, Sr., runs a family-owned liquor store. His mother, Judy (Butler) Shea, is a volunteer emergency medical technician (EMT). Jim has one sister, Sarah.

YOUTH

Shea grew up in West Hartford as part of an extended family of athletes. In fact, both his father and grandfather competed in the Olympics. His grandfather, John ("Jack") Shea, won two gold medals as a speed skater at the 1932 Winter Olympic Games in Lake Placid, New York. Jack Shea also worked as an Olympic organizer and helped bring the Games back to Lake Placid in 1980.

Shea's father, Jim Shea, Sr., competed in three Nordic (cross-country) skiing events at the 1964 Winter Olympic Games in Innsbruck, Austria. He also coached the U.S. biathlon team at the 1972 Winter Olympic Games in Sapporo, Japan. In addition, Shea's mother was an outstanding alpine skier who just missed making the 1964 Olympic team. She finished seventh in the Olympic trials, but only the top six athletes made the team.

Despite their athletic talent, the Shea family never pushed Jim Jr. to follow in their footsteps. Although he was inspired by the examples of his father and grandfather, neither of their chosen sports appealed to him. He never really thought about competing in the Olympics until 1980, when he attended the Games in Lake Placid and watched the U.S. Hockey Team defeat a powerful Russian squad in a game called the "Miracle on Ice." But it took Shea many years to find the sport that would lead him to Olympic glory.

Shea was an adventurous teenager who was always seeking an adrenaline rush. He experimented with a number of different dangerous activities over the years. For example, he went "urban surfing" by standing on the hood of a moving car. He also enjoyed dirt biking and jumping into lakes from the tops of cliffs.

EDUCATION

Shea struggled in school because he suffered from dyslexia, a type of learning disability in which the brain mixes up letters and numbers. He found reading very difficult, and he was terrified of being asked to read aloud in front of the class. Some of his classmates made fun of him, which led to problems with low self-esteem and depression. Shea reacted to these problems by indulging in self-destructive behavior, like drinking alcohol and performing dangerous stunts.

Shea's academic struggles continued at Conard High School in West Hartford. But he soon found that participating in sports made him more popular among his fellow students and provided him with a release for his

Shea (center) stands with his grandfather, Jack Shea (left), and his father, Jim Shea, Sr. (right), after becoming the first third-generation Olympic athlete. This picture was taken in Lake Placid after Jim Shea placed second in the 2001 World Cup men's skeleton competition and earned a spot on the 2002 U.S. Olympic team.

negative feelings. He played goalie on the varsity lacrosse team and defenseman on the varsity hockey squad. Shortly after graduating from high school, Shea moved with his family to Lake Placid, New York. He took classes at North Country College in the mid-1990s, but he ended up putting his studies on hold to concentrate on the sport of skeleton.

CAREER HIGHLIGHTS

Becoming Involved in the Sport of Skeleton

Shea became involved in the relatively unknown sport of skeleton through a series of coincidences. One year, while he was visiting his grandfather at his home in Lake Placid, Shea could hear announcements over the loudspeakers at the nearby Olympic bobsledding facility. It occurred to him then that he might like to try bobsledding someday. In 1988, when he was 20 years old, he moved with his family to Lake Placid. For the first few years, he spent his days skiing or snowboarding and worked at night as a restaurant cook or bartender. He eventually met some people who were involved in bobsledding and got a chance to try the sport. He ended up competing in bobsledding for two years, first as a brakeman and then as a driver, but had little success. Although he enjoyed bobsledding, he found it too expensive (a single sled can cost more than $45,000) and began looking for a new sport.

Shea tried the sport of skeleton for the first time in 1994. In skeleton, riders speed down a steep, twisting bobsled track on a lightweight, three-foot-long steel sled. The sport is similar to luge, except that competitors ride the sleds while lying on their stomachs and go down the hill head-first. Skeleton sleds have no brakes or steering mechanisms. Riders steer by subtly moving their heads and shoulders or occasionally by dragging a toe. The sleds typically approach speeds of 80 miles per hour, and riders often experience forces over four times the strength of gravity (four Gs). Despite the high speeds, skeleton riders wear skintight lycra-spandex suits with little padding. "I don't wear any padding, because if I make a mistake, I want to remember it," Shea stated. "In a bobsled you bang into the wall, and you don't feel anything." Skeleton riders also wear aerodynamic helmets, the chins of which are just inches above the snow. The sport requires speed, power, agility, strength, and coordination.

On Shea's first skeleton ride, he says, "The first time I went down, I scared myself half to death, but my immediate reaction was, How fast can I get back to the top? For an adrenaline junkie like me, there's no bigger high. It was a wicked challenge, and just a great experience."

Skeleton originated in the 1880s and is considered the world's first sliding sport. The name "skeleton" may come from the German word *Schlitten,* which means sled. Some people claim that the sport got its name from the skeleton-like design of the sleds, which consist of a steel frame and two narrow runners. Of course, competitors like to offer their own explanations. "Bobsledders used to call it skeleton, because it's a skeleton of a bobsled, and we break a lot of bones," Shea joked. The sport is very popular in parts of Europe. In fact, it was featured in the Winter Olympics when the Games were held in St. Moritz, Switzerland, in 1926 and 1948.

On Shea's first skeleton ride, the sled flew out from under him on a turn. He landed on his rear end and slid until he had shredded both his suit and his leg. Nevertheless, he was hooked on the dangerous sport. "The first time I went down, I scared myself half to death, but my immediate reaction was, How fast can I get back to the top?" he recalled. "For an adrenaline junkie like me, there's no bigger high. It was a wicked challenge, and just a great experience."

Shea also loved the relatively inexpensive nature of the sport (a beginning sled costs only a few hundred dollars). Though he admits that skeleton is dangerous, he claims that most injuries are minor. "No one's ever died in the sport, crazy as it looks," he noted. "Sliders are a bunch of guys who like to scare themselves. We travel at 80 miles per hour on ice with very little steering. Blood is a common sight on the track. But it is also very, very, exciting."

"I was either going to do it right or I'd quit. I spent the next two months hauling my 70-pound sled and a hockey bag full of clothes through Europe. I'd hitchhike or get rides from the Brits [skeleton racers from Great Britain], who called me their pet Yank [Yankee]. One of them gave me his old sled. I lived on $325 for two months, eating bread and hot dogs with lots of mustard. I didn't shower for three weeks at a time and would sleep in a four-man bobsled in the storage sheds. But I found my way to the tracks."

Pushing to Be a World Class Skeleton Rider

Shea became a member of the U.S. Skeleton Team in 1995, which allowed him to compete in World Cup events around the world. The World Cup is the top level of international skeleton competition. He sold his Jeep for traveling expenses and began competing in Europe in 1996. At first Shea found himself totally outclassed by his European rivals. "I had my hunting jacket and moon boots on, and I wore golf shoes on the track," he recalled. "I didn't know what I was doing." It took some time before Shea fit in with his fellow competitors. In fact, members of the Austrian team would not even acknowledge him during his first year in international competition. Shea did manage to win the U.S. National Championships at Lake Placid in 1996 and earn U.S. Skeleton rookie of the year honors.

Shea continued to perform poorly in international competition the following year. He struggled with a number of problems, including a lack of money, a broken sled, and little understanding of foreign languages. Despite these problems, he knew that he could not quit skeleton before he

Shea pushes off during the men's skeleton finals at the 2002 Olympics.

had given the sport his best effort. He decided to remain in Europe for several months of intensive training. "I was either going to do it right or I'd quit," he recalled. "I spent the next two months hauling my 70-pound sled and a hockey bag full of clothes through Europe. I'd hitchhike or get rides from the Brits [skeleton racers from Great Britain], who called me their pet

141

Yank [Yankee]. One of them gave me his old sled. I lived on $325 for two months, eating bread and hot dogs with lots of mustard. I didn't shower for three weeks at a time and would sleep in a four-man bobsled in the storage sheds. But I found my way to the tracks."

Shea's determination and perseverance earned the respect of his fellow competitors and also led to rapid improvements in his skeleton skills. In January 1998 he became the first American ever to win a World Cup skeleton event. He went on to be the top U.S. finisher in every World Cup race that season. In February 1999 Shea shocked many people by winning the Skeleton World Championships in Altenberg, Germany. He thus became the first — and still the only — American to do so. He remembered that his feat was so unexpected that race officials "didn't even have an American flag to hang up."

> "
>
> *Shea is the first third-generation Olympian in the history of the Winter Games. "I'm really excited to have this tradition. To be able to follow in my grandfather's and my father's footsteps is a great honor. My family has never pushed me. When I made the national team for the first time, I remember telling my grandfather, 'I'm going to go off and get you a medal and make you proud of me.' And he said, 'Well, I'm already proud of you, Jim.'"*
>
> "

Shea proved that his 1999 world title was no fluke when he finished third at the 2000 World Championships. He also won a gold medal at the inaugural Winter Goodwill Games in Lake Placid that year, and he finished third in the World Cup standings for the 2000-01 season. As Shea established himself as one of the top competitors on the international skeleton scene, many people began asking him to help convince the International Olympic Committee (IOC) to include skeleton as a medal sport at the 2002 Winter Games in Salt Lake City, Utah. Excited about the possibility of following in the footsteps of his Olympian father and grandfather, Shea worked hard to get skeleton recognized as an Olympic sport. "I would knock on every outhouse, doghouse, henhouse," he stated. Shea even took the president of the Salt Lake Olympic Organizing Committee, Mitt Romney, for a ride on his skeleton to expose him to the thrill of the sport. Recognizing skeleton's potential appeal to younger viewers, the IOC ultimately decided to add skeleton to the 2002 Olympic program. "People think it's great. They think it's nuts," Shea noted. "When people see it at the Olympics, they're going to love it."

Becoming the First Third-Generation Winter Olympian

Shea clinched a spot on the U.S. Olympic Team in December 2001 with a second-place finish in a World Cup event. He thus became the first third-generation Olympian in the history of the Winter Games. "I'm really excited to have this tradition. To be able to follow in my grandfather's and my father's footsteps is a great honor," he stated. "My family has never pushed me. When I made the national team for the first time, I remember telling my grandfather, 'I'm going to go off and get you a medal and make you proud of me.' And he said, 'Well, I'm already proud of you, Jim.'"

As the 2002 Winter Games approached, Shea and his father and grandfather became the focus of a great deal of media attention. All three men appeared in several television commercials for the Sprint telephone company. At the age of 91, Jack Shea was the oldest living Winter Olympics gold medalist. Speed Skating USA—the governing body of the sport in America—had named an award after him. The lively old man even carried the Olympic torch as it passed through Lake Placid as part of a cross-country relay on its way to Salt Lake City. In numerous interviews, Jack Shea spoke eloquently about the higher purpose of the Olympics. "A

Shea screams through a turn during the men's skeleton finals at the 2002 Olympics.

friendly gathering between nations in which countries come together in the spirit of peace, that's the Olympic ideal," he said. "There's never been a time when that ideal wasn't worth striving for. The people who come to the Games are really carriers. They carry home, like spokes from the hub of a wheel, everything they've seen and learned at the Olympics."

———— ❝ ————

"My grandfather used to dream about me competing in the Olympics. When I qualified for the Games, he could not have been more proud. This is not about the gold medals. It's about competing. That's what my grandfather always used to say. It's about taking part. This is a great thing when the world comes together in a peaceful, friendly competition. That's what the Olympics are all about — representing your country with honor and grace."

———— ❞ ————

Sadly, Jack Shea was killed just a few weeks before he would have seen his grandson compete in the Olympics. He died of internal injuries one day after being involved in a head-on automobile accident just a few blocks from his home in Lake Placid. According to police, the other driver was legally drunk at the time of the crash. Jim Shea, Jr. flew home from Salt Lake City for his grandfather's funeral. "This is a great loss to my family," he stated. "I'm just glad I had him around as long as I did." The Shea family draped an Olympic flag over the casket and drove the funeral procession around the ice track in Lake Placid where Jack Shea had won his gold medals 70 years earlier. The U.S. Olympic Committee awarded Jack Shea its highest honor, the Olympic Torch Award, shortly after his death.

Although Jim Shea, Jr. was deeply saddened by the loss of his grandfather, he was determined to honor his memory at the Olympics. "My grandfather used to dream about me competing in the Olympics. When I qualified for the Games, he could not have been more proud," he recalled. "This is not about the gold medals. It's about competing. That's what my grandfather always used to say. It's about taking part. This is a great thing when the world comes together in a peaceful, friendly competition. That's what the Olympics are all about — representing your country with honor and grace." Shea was honored when his American teammates selected him to recite the Olympic oath in the opening ceremony—just as his grandfather had done 70 years earlier. Along with his father, he also helped carry the torch that was used to light the Olympic flame.

Winning a Gold Medal in Skeleton at the 2002 Winter Olympics

The Olympic skeleton course in Salt Lake City was 4,380 feet long, dropped 340 vertical feet, and featured 16 turns. Skeleton athletes completed two runs down the course, and the competitors with the lowest combined times for the two runs won the Olympic medals. The skeleton races took place on February 20. Over 15,000 fans lined the sides and bottom of the course on race day. Many people in the crowd held up signs supporting Shea.

Shea competed with an American flag painted on his sled and a bald eagle painted on his helmet. He posted the lowest time in the first run to take control of first place. "I just tried to concentrate on the basics," he remembered. "There's so much going on. There were 15,000 screaming people. I was just having a blast." Competitors made their second runs in reverse order, meaning that Shea would go last. Unfortunately, it began to snow during the second run. This usually puts later sliders at a disadvantage, as fresh snow tends to make the icy track slower.

As Shea prepared to make his final run, defending world champion Martin Rettl of Austria sat in first place, Gregor Staehli of Switzerland was second, and Clifton Wrottesley of Ireland was third. After running along and pushing his sled for the first 50 yards, Shea dove onto the skeleton and assumed an aerodynamic sliding position. Though his second run was fast, the first three split times showed him trailing Rettl by 0.1 seconds. The pro-American crowd grew quiet, expecting Shea to narrowly miss the gold medal. But he somehow made up time in the last turn. When the final scores were posted, Shea had won the gold medal by 0.05 seconds, with a combined time of 1:41.96. His family believes that his grandfather "gave him a little push" near the finish line. "I definitely felt him here today," Jim Jr. said later. "He had some unfinished business before he went on to heaven. Now he can go."

Shea struggled to stop his sled after the gold-medal run and finally fell off because he was so excited. The first people to run up and congratulate him were his fellow competitors—Rettl, Staehli, and Wrottesley. Shea's win had bumped Wrottesley off the podium and prevented him from winning Ireland's first-ever Winter Olympics medal. Nevertheless, Wrottesley said afterward, "I was completely elated. The right man won." Staehli, the

Olympic men's skeleton champion Jim Shea (center) poses with silver medal winner Martin Rettl (right) of Austria and bronze medal winner Gregor Staehli (left) of Switzerland.

bronze medalist, added that "We are all a big family. It's great to be on the podium with Jim. It's cool. I'm very happy with what happened in our sport today."

After being congratulated by his competitors, Shea pulled a picture of his grandfather out of his helmet and waved it before the crowd, which began shouting "U-S-Shea! U-S-Shea!"in honor of his accomplishment. "I had a lot of fans in the crowd. My sponsors were there, my parents, my family and friends. It was very emotional. I had so many people who helped me get where I am today. To have my fellow competitors come up to me meant the most," Shea stated. "Now that I have the gold medal I can honestly say the friendships are more important. Gregor's dad is so supportive of me. I can't go to Innsbruck without getting a home-cooked meal from Martin's mom. We're not the only ones. It's about the world coming together in a great, peaceful way." Later the same day, Americans Tristan Gale and Lea Ann Parsley won the gold and silver medals in the women's skeleton competition.

Sharing His Success

In the weeks following his gold-medal performance, Shea gave numerous interviews and made lots of public appearances. He also started the Shea

Foundation to raise money for equipment and coaches to help more kids participate in sports. "With kids having so many problems growing up today, if I can bring them out to the skeleton track and to speed skating and jumping and just sports, in general, they can overcome their fears in sports," he explained. "They're going to be able to take that ability to overcome difficult fears and challenges and carry it on to life and make good decisions in life."

Shea realizes that he was lucky to discover skeleton and follow the sport to the Olympic Games. He draws from his own experience in advising future Olympic hopefuls to "be smart about it and don't give up. Be very persistent. Take your time and do it right. It doesn't come overnight. There's a million obstacles in the way, but the only thing that's going to stop them is themselves."

HOME AND FAMILY

Shea lives and trains in Lake Placid, New York. Though he is not married, he has been dating Jessie Colby for some time. He remains very close to his parents as well as his extended family.

—— " ——

"I had a lot of fans in the crowd. My sponsors were there, my parents, my family and friends. It was very emotional. I had so many people who helped me get where I am today. To have my fellow competitors come up to me [after the race] meant the most. Now that I have the gold medal I can honestly say the friendships are more important."

—— " ——

HOBBIES AND OTHER INTERESTS

In his spare time, Shea enjoys playing polo, waterskiing, and riding motorcycles and snowmobiles. "Anything that scares me, I guess," he said of his hobbies. Shea also serves as a volunteer firefighter in Lake Placid.

HONORS AND AWARDS

U.S. Skeleton Rookie of the Year: 1996
U.S. National Championship Skeleton: 1996, First Place
World Championship Skeleton: 1999, First Place; 2000, Third Place
Winter Goodwill Games Skeleton: 2000, Gold Medal
Olympic Skeleton: 2002, Gold Medal
YMCA Man of the Year: 2002

FURTHER READING

Periodicals

Boston Herald, Jan. 27, 2002, p.B33

Colorado Springs Gazette, Feb. 11, 2001, p.SP10; Jan. 23, 2002, p.SP1; Feb. 20, 2002, Olympics sec., p.3; Feb. 21, 2002, Olympics sec., p.1

Hartford (Conn.) Courant, Feb. 21, 2000, p.C1

Houston Chronicle, Feb. 21, 2002, p.1

Los Angeles Times, Jan. 23, 2002, p.D1; Feb. 20, 2002, p.U5

New York Times, Jan. 23, 2002, p.A16; Feb. 5, 2002, p.G6; Feb. 21, 2002, p.A1

People, Feb. 11, 2002, p.77

Sports Illustrated, Dec. 17, 2001, p.106; Feb. 7, 2002, p.75

Sports Illustrated for Kids, Feb. 1, 2002, p.47; May 2002, p.6

Online Articles

http://news.bbc.co.uk/winterolympics2002/low/english/luge_and_skeleton/ (*BBC News,* 2 articles: "Emotional Gold for Shea" and "Tearful Triumph Cheers America," Feb. 20, 2002)

http://cbs.sportsline.com/b/page/pressbox/0,1328,5036044,00.html (*CBS Sports Online,* "Shea Jr. Captures Olympic Spirit with Golden Run," Feb. 20, 2002)

http://olympics.belointeractive.com/skeleton (*Dallas Morning News Online,* "Shea's Chief Motivation," Feb. 21, 2002)

Online Databases

Biography Resource Center Online, 2002

ADDRESS

Jim Shea, Jr.
U.S. Bobsled and Skeleton Federation
421 Old Military Road
Lake Placid, NY 12946

WORLD WIDE WEB SITES

http://www.usbsf.com
http://www.olympic-usa.org
http://sports.yahoo.com/oly/skeleton/usoc/bios/m/j_shea.html

Photo and Illustration Credits

Simon Ammann/Photos: AP/Wide World Photos; copyright © Reuters New Media Inc./CORBIS; AP/Wide World Photos.

Shannon Bahrke/Photos: Copyright © 2002/Jonathan Selkowitz; Jeff J. Mitchell/Reuters/TIMEPIX; AP/Wide World Photos; Petar Kujundzic/Reuters/TIMEPIX.

Kelly Clark/Photos: Copyright © 2002/Tom Zilkas; AP/Wide World Photos.

Vonetta Flowers/Photos: AP/Wide World Photos; Jim Bourg/Reuters/TIME-PIX.

Cammi Granato/Photos: USA Hockey/Gerry Thomas; Brian Hill/TIMEPIX; AP/Wide World Photos.

Chris Klug/Photos: Jay LaPrete for the National Kidney Foundation; AP/Wide World Photos; Jeff J. Mitchell/Reuters/TIMEPIX; Petar Kujundzic/Reuters/TIMEPIX; AP/Wide World Photos.

Jonny Moseley/Photos: J. Emilio Flores/Getty Images; Nathan Bilow/Getty Images; Al Bello/Getty Images.

Apolo Ohno/Photos: Copyright © Reuters NewMedia Inc./CORBIS; Jerry Lampen/Reuters/TIMEPIX; AP/Wide World Photos; Kimimasa Mayama/Reuters/TIMEPIX.

Sylke Otto/Photos: AP/Wide World Photos.

Ryne Sanborn/Photos: Copyright © Tribune Media Services, Inc. All Rights Reserved. Reprinted with permission; David Gray/Reuters/ TIMEPIX; Mike Blake/Reuters/TIMEPIX.

Jim Shea, Jr./Photos: AP/Wide World Photos; Petar Kujundzic/Reuters/TIMEPIX; Jim Bourg/Reuters/TIMEPIX.

How to Use the Cumulative Index

Our indexes have a new look. In an effort to make our indexes easier to use, we've combined the Name and General Index into a new, Cumulative Index. This single ready-reference resource covers all the volumes in *Biography Today*, both the general series and the special subject series. The new Cumulative Index contains complete listings of all individuals who have appeared in *Biography Today* since the series began. Their names appear in bold-faced type, followed by the issue in which they appear. The Cumulative Index also includes references for the occupations, nationalities, and ethnic and minority origins of individuals profiled in *Biography Today*.

We have also made some changes to our specialty indexes, the Places of Birth Index and the Birthday Index. To consolidate and to save space, the Places of Birth Index and the Birthday Index will no longer appear in the January and April issues of the softbound subscription series. But these indexes can still be found in the September issue of the softbound subscription series, in the hardbound Annual Cumulation at the end of each year, and in each volume of the special subject series.

General Series

The General Series of *Biography Today* is denoted in the index with the month and year of the issue in which the individual appeared. Each individual also appears in the Annual Cumulation for that year.

Special Subject Series

The Special Subject Series of *Biography Today* are each denoted in the index with an abbreviated form of the series name, plus the number of the volume in which the individual appears. They are listed as follows.

Adams, Ansel .... Artist V.1	(Artists Series)
Cabot, Meg................. Author V.12	(Author Series)
Fauci, Anthony.............. Science V.7	(Scientists & Inventors Series)
Moseley, Jonny .... Sport V.8	(Sports Series)
Peterson, Roger Tory .... WorLdr V.1	(World Leaders Series: Environmental Leaders)
Sadat, Anwar .... WorLdr V.2	(World Leaders Series: Modern African Leaders)
Wolf, Hazel................. WorLdr V.3	(World Leaders Series: Environmental Leaders 2)

Updates

Updated information on selected individuals appears in the Appendix at the end of the *Biography Today* Annual Cumulation. In the index, the original entry is listed first, followed by any updates.

Arafat, Yasir .... Sep 94; Update 94;
  Update 95; Update 96; Update 97; Update 98;
  Update 00; Update 01; Update 02
Gates, Bill .... Apr 93; Update 98;
  Update 00; Science V.5; Update 01
Griffith Joyner, Florence......... Sport V.1;
  Update 98
Sanders, Barry .... Sep 95; Update 99
Spock, Dr. Benjamin .... Sep 95; Update 98
Yeltsin, Boris .... Apr 92; Update 93;
  Update 95; Update 96; Update 98; Update 00

Cumulative Index

This cumulative index includes names, occupations, nationalities, and ethnic and minority origins that pertain to all individuals profiled in *Biography Today* since the debut of the series in 1992.

Places of Birth Index

The following index lists the places of birth for the individuals profiled in *Biography Today*. Places of birth are entered under state, province, and/or country.

Birthday Index

February (continued)	Year
6 Leakey, Mary	1913
Rosa, Emily	1987
Zmeskal, Kim	1976
7 Brooks, Garth	1962
Wang, An	1920
Wilder, Laura Ingalls	1867
8 Grisham, John	1955
9 Love, Susan	1948
10 Konigsburg, E.L.	1930
Norman, Greg	1955
11 Aniston, Jennifer	1969
Brandy	1979
Rowland, Kelly	1981
Yolen, Jane	1939
12 Blume, Judy	1938
Kurzweil, Raymond	1948
Small, David	1945
Woodson, Jacqueline	?1964
13 Moss, Randy	1977
Sleator, William	1945
15 Groening, Matt	1954
Jagr, Jaromir	1972
Sones, Sonya	1952
Van Dyken, Amy	1973
16 Freeman, Cathy	1973
17 Anderson, Marian	1897
Hargreaves, Alison	1962
Jordan, Michael	1963
18 Morrison, Toni	1931
19 Tan, Amy	1952
20 Adams, Ansel	1902
Barkley, Charles	1963
Cobain, Kurt	1967
Crawford, Cindy	1966
Hernandez, Livan	1975
Littrell, Brian	1975
21 Carpenter, Mary Chapin	1958
Hewitt, Jennifer Love	1979
Jordan, Barbara	1936
Mugabe, Robert	1924
22 Barrymore, Drew	1975
Fernandez, Lisa	1971
23 Brown, Claude	1937
24 Jobs, Steven	1955
Vernon, Mike	1963
Whitestone, Heather	1973
25 Voigt, Cynthia	1942
26 Thompson, Jenny	1973

	Year
27 Clinton, Chelsea	1980
Hunter-Gault, Charlayne	1942
28 Andretti, Mario	1940
Pauling, Linus	1901

March	Year
1 Ellison, Ralph Waldo	1914
Murie, Olaus J.	1889
Nielsen, Jerri	1952
Rabin, Yitzhak	1922
Zamora, Pedro	1972
2 Gorbachev, Mikhail	1931
Satcher, David	1941
Seuss, Dr.	1904
3 Hooper, Geoff	1979
Joyner-Kersee, Jackie	1962
MacLachlan, Patricia	1938
4 Armstrong, Robb	1962
Morgan, Garrett	1877
5 Margulis, Lynn	1938
6 Ashley, Maurice	1966
7 McCarty, Oseola	1908
8 Prinze, Freddie Jr.	1976
10 Guy, Jasmine	1964
Miller, Shannon	1977
Wolf, Hazel	1898
12 Hamilton, Virginia	1936
Nye, Naomi Shihab	1952
13 Van Meter, Vicki	1982
14 Dayne, Ron	1977
Hanson, Taylor	1983
Williamson, Kevin	1965
15 Ginsburg, Ruth Bader	1933
White, Ruth	1942
16 O'Neal, Shaquille	1972
17 Hamm, Mia	1972
Nureyev, Rudolf	1938
18 Blair, Bonnie	1964
de Klerk, F.W.	1936
Griese, Brian	1975
Queen Latifah	1970
19 Blanchard, Rachel	1976
20 Lee, Spike	1957
Lowry, Lois	1937
Sachar, Louis	1954
21 Gilbert, Walter	1932
O'Donnell, Rosie	1962
22 Shatner, William	1931
24 Manning, Peyton	1976

BIRTHDAY INDEX

Biography Today
General Series

For ages 9 and above

"Biography Today **will be useful in elementary and middle school libraries and in public library children's collections where there is a need for biographies of current personalities. High schools serving reluctant readers may also want to consider a subscription."**

— *Booklist,* American Library Association

"Highly recommended for the young adult audience. Readers will delight in the accessible, energetic, tell-all style; teachers, librarians, and parents will welcome the clever format, intelligent and informative text. It should prove especially useful in motivating 'reluctant' readers or literate nonreaders."

— *MultiCultural Review*

"Written in a friendly, almost chatty tone, the profiles offer quick, objective information. While coverage of current figures makes *Biography Today* a useful reference tool, an appealing format and wide scope make it a fun resource to browse." — *School Library Journal*

"The best source for current information at a level kids can understand."

— Kelly Bryant, School Librarian, Carlton, OR

"Easy for kids to read. We love it! Don't want to be without it."

— Lynn McWhirter, School Librarian, Rockford, IL

Biography Today **General Series** includes a unique combination of current biographical profiles that teachers and librarians — and the readers themselves — tell us are most appealing. The **General Series** is available as a 3-issue subscription; hardcover annual cumulation; or subscription plus cumulation.

Within the **General Series**, your readers will find a variety of sketches about:

- Authors
- Musicians
- Political leaders
- Sports figures
- Movie actresses & actors
- Cartoonists
- Scientists
- Astronauts
- TV personalities
- and the movers & shakers in many other fields!

ONE-YEAR SUBSCRIPTION
- 3 softcover issues, 6" x 9"
- Published in January, April, and September
- 1-year subscription, $57
- 150 pages per issue
- 8-10 profiles per issue
- Contact sources for additional information
- Cumulative General, Places of Birth, and Birthday Indexes

HARDBOUND ANNUAL CUMULATION
- Sturdy 6" x 9" hardbound volume
- Published in December
- $58 per volume
- 450 pages per volume
- 25-30 profiles — includes all profiles found in softcover issues for that calendar year
- Cumulative General, Places of Birth, and Birthday Indexes
- Special appendix features current updates of previous profiles

SUBSCRIPTION AND CUMULATION COMBINATION
- $99 for 3 softcover issues plus the hardbound volume

1992

Paula Abdul
Andre Agassi
Kirstie Alley
Terry Anderson
Roseanne Arnold
Isaac Asimov
James Baker
Charles Barkley
Larry Bird
Judy Blume
Berke Breathed
Garth Brooks
Barbara Bush
George Bush
Fidel Castro
Bill Clinton
Bill Cosby
Diana, Princess of Wales
Shannen Doherty
Elizabeth Dole
David Duke
Gloria Estefan
Mikhail Gorbachev
Steffi Graf
Wayne Gretzky
Matt Groening
Alex Haley
Hammer
Martin Handford
Stephen Hawking
Hulk Hogan
Saddam Hussein
Lee Iacocca
Bo Jackson
Mae Jemison
Peter Jennings
Steven Jobs
Pope John Paul II
Magic Johnson
Michael Jordon
Jackie Joyner-Kersee
Spike Lee
Mario Lemieux
Madeleine L'Engle
Jay Leno
Yo-Yo Ma
Nelson Mandela
Wynton Marsalis
Thurgood Marshall
Ann Martin
Barbara McClintock
Emily Arnold McCully
Antonia Novello
Sandra Day O'Connor
Rosa Parks

Jane Pauley
H. Ross Perot
Luke Perry
Scottie Pippen
Colin Powell
Jason Priestley
Queen Latifah
Yitzhak Rabin
Sally Ride
Pete Rose
Nolan Ryan
H. Norman
   Schwarzkopf
Jerry Seinfeld
Dr. Seuss
Gloria Steinem
Clarence Thomas
Chris Van Allsburg
Cynthia Voigt
Bill Watterson
Robin Williams
Oprah Winfrey
Kristi Yamaguchi
Boris Yeltsin

1993

Maya Angelou
Arthur Ashe
Avi
Kathleen Battle
Candice Bergen
Boutros Boutros-Ghali
Chris Burke
Dana Carvey
Cesar Chavez
Henry Cisneros
Hillary Rodham Clinton
Jacques Cousteau
Cindy Crawford
Macaulay Culkin
Lois Duncan
Marian Wright Edelman
Cecil Fielder
Bill Gates
Sara Gilbert
Dizzy Gillespie
Al Gore
Cathy Guisewite
Jasmine Guy
Anita Hill
Ice-T
Darci Kistler
k.d. lang
Dan Marino
Rigoberta Menchu
Walter Dean Myers

Martina Navratilova
Phyllis Reynolds Naylor
Rudolf Nureyev
Shaquille O'Neal
Janet Reno
Jerry Rice
Mary Robinson
Winona Ryder
Jerry Spinelli
Denzel Washington
Keenen Ivory Wayans
Dave Winfield

1994

Tim Allen
Marian Anderson
Mario Andretti
Ned Andrews
Yasir Arafat
Bruce Babbitt
Mayim Bialik
Bonnie Blair
Ed Bradley
John Candy
Mary Chapin Carpenter
Benjamin Chavis
Connie Chung
Beverly Cleary
Kurt Cobain
F.W. de Klerk
Rita Dove
Linda Ellerbee
Sergei Fedorov
Zlata Filipovic
Daisy Fuentes
Ruth Bader Ginsburg
Whoopi Goldberg
Tonya Harding
Melissa Joan Hart
Geoff Hooper
Whitney Houston
Dan Jansen
Nancy Kerrigan
Alexi Lalas
Charlotte Lopez
Wilma Mankiller
Shannon Miller
Toni Morrison
Richard Nixon
Greg Norman
Severo Ochoa
River Phoenix
Elizabeth Pine
Jonas Salk
Richard Scarry
Emmitt Smith

Will Smith
Steven Spielberg
Patrick Stewart
R.L. Stine
Lewis Thomas
Barbara Walters
Charlie Ward
Steve Young
Kim Zmeskal

1995

Troy Aikman
Jean-Bertrand Aristide
Oksana Baiul
Halle Berry
Benazir Bhutto
Jonathan Brandis
Warren E. Burger
Ken Burns
Candace Cameron
Jimmy Carter
Agnes de Mille
Placido Domingo
Janet Evans
Patrick Ewing
Newt Gingrich
John Goodman
Amy Grant
Jesse Jackson
James Earl Jones
Julie Krone
David Letterman
Rush Limbaugh
Heather Locklear
Reba McEntire
Joe Montana
Cosmas Ndeti
Hakeem Olajuwon
Ashley Olsen
Mary-Kate Olsen
Jennifer Parkinson
Linus Pauling
Itzhak Perlman
Cokie Roberts
Wilma Rudolph
Salt 'N' Pepa
Barry Sanders
William Shatner
Elizabeth George
   Speare
Dr. Benjamin Spock
Jonathan Taylor
   Thomas
Vicki Van Meter
Heather Whitestone
Pedro Zamora

1996

Aung San Suu Kyi
Boyz II Men
Brandy
Ron Brown
Mariah Carey
Jim Carrey
Larry Champagne III
Christo
Chelsea Clinton
Coolio
Bob Dole
David Duchovny
Debbi Fields
Chris Galeczka
Jerry Garcia
Jennie Garth
Wendy Guey
Tom Hanks
Alison Hargreaves
Sir Edmund Hillary
Judith Jamison
Barbara Jordan
Annie Leibovitz
Carl Lewis
Jim Lovell
Mickey Mantle
Lynn Margulis
Iqbal Masih
Mark Messier
Larisa Oleynik
Christopher Pike
David Robinson
Dennis Rodman
Selena
Monica Seles
Don Shula
Kerri Strug
Tiffani-Amber Thiessen
Dave Thomas
Jaleel White

1997

Madeleine Albright
Marcus Allen
Gillian Anderson
Rachel Blanchard
Zachery Ty Bryan
Adam Ezra Cohen
Claire Danes
Celine Dion
Jean Driscoll
Louis Farrakhan
Ella Fitzgerald

Harrison Ford
Bryant Gumbel
John Johnson
Michael Johnson
Maya Lin
George Lucas
John Madden
Bill Monroe
Alanis Morissette
Sam Morrison
Rosie O'Donnell
Muammar el-Qaddafi
Christopher Reeve
Pete Sampras
Pat Schroeder
Rebecca Sealfon
Tupac Shakur
Tabitha Soren
Herbert Tarvin
Merlin Tuttle
Mara Wilson

1998

Bella Abzug
Kofi Annan
Neve Campbell
Sean Combs (Puff
   Daddy)
Dalai Lama (Tenzin
   Gyatso)
Diana, Princess of Wales
Leonardo DiCaprio
Walter E. Diemer
Ruth Handler
Hanson
Livan Hernandez
Jewel
Jimmy Johnson
Tara Lipinski
Jody-Anne Maxwell
Dominique Moceanu
Alexandra Nechita
Brad Pitt
LeAnn Rimes
Emily Rosa
David Satcher
Betty Shabazz
Kordell Stewart
Shinichi Suzuki
Mother Teresa
Mike Vernon
Reggie White
Kate Winslet

1999

Ben Affleck
Jennifer Aniston
Maurice Ashley
Kobe Bryant
Bessie Delany
Sadie Delany
Sharon Draper
Sarah Michelle Gellar
John Glenn
Savion Glover
Jeff Gordon
David Hampton
Lauryn Hill
King Hussein
Lynn Johnston
Shari Lewis
Oseola McCarty
Mark McGwire
Slobodan Milosevic
Natalie Portman
J. K. Rowling
Frank Sinatra
Gene Siskel
Sammy Sosa
John Stanford
Natalia Toro
Shania Twain
Mitsuko Uchida
Jesse Ventura
Venus Williams

2000

Christina Aguilera
K.A. Applegate
Lance Armstrong
Backstreet Boys
Daisy Bates
Harry Blackmun
George W. Bush
Carson Daly
Ron Dayne
Henry Louis Gates, Jr.
Doris Haddock
   (Granny D)
Jennifer Love Hewitt
Chamique Holdsclaw
Katie Holmes
Charlayne Hunter-Gault
Johanna Johnson
Craig Kielburger
John Lasseter
Peyton Manning
Ricky Martin
John McCain
Walter Payton
Freddie Prinze, Jr.

Viviana Risca
Briana Scurry
George Thampy
CeCe Winans

2001

Jessica Alba
Christiane Amanpour
Drew Barrymore
Jeff Bezos
Destiny's Child
Dale Earnhardt
Carly Fiorina
Aretha Franklin
Cathy Freeman
Tony Hawk
Faith Hill
Kim Dae-jung
Madeleine L'Engle
Mariangela Lisanti
Frankie Muniz
*N Sync
Ellen Ochoa
Jeff Probst
Julia Roberts
Carl T. Rowan
Britney Spears
Chris Tucker
Lloyd D. Ward
Alan Webb
Chris Weinke

2002

Aaliyah
Osama bin Laden
Mary J. Blige
Aubyn Burnside
Aaron Carter
Julz Chavez
Dick Cheney
Hilary Duff
Billy Gilman
Rudolph Giuliani
Brian Griese
Jennifer Lopez
Dave Mirra
Dineh Mohajer
Leanne Nakamura
Daniel Radcliffe
Condoleezza Rice
Marla Runyan
Ruth Simmons
Mattie Stepanek
J.R.R. Tolkien
Barry Watson
Tyrone Willingham
Elijah Wood

Biography Today

For ages 9 and above

Subject Series

AUTHOR SERIES

"A useful tool for children's assignment needs." — *School Library Journal*

"The prose is workmanlike: report writers will find enough detail to begin sound investigations, and browsers are likely to find someone of interest." — *School Library Journal*

SCIENTISTS & INVENTORS SERIES

"The articles are readable, attractively laid out, and touch on important points that will suit assignment needs. Browsers will note the clear writing and interesting details." — *School Library Journal*

"The book is excellent for demonstrating that scientists are real people with widely diverse backgrounds and personal interests. The biographies are fascinating to read." — *The Science Teacher*

SPORTS SERIES

"This series should become a standard resource in libraries that serve intermediate students." — *School Library Journal*

ENVIRONMENTAL LEADERS #1

"A tremendous book that fills a gap in the biographical category of books. This is a great reference book." — *Science Scope*

Expands and complements the General Series and targets specific subject areas . . .

Our readers asked for it! They wanted more biographies, and the *Biography Today* **Subject Series** is our response to that demand. Now your readers can choose their special areas of interest and go on to read about their favorites in those fields. Priced at just $39 per volume, the following specific volumes are included in the *Biography Today* **Subject Series**:

- **Artists Series**
- **Author Series**
- **Scientists & Inventors Series**
- **Sports Series**
- **World Leaders Series**
  Environmental Leaders
  Modern African Leaders

FEATURES AND FORMAT

- Sturdy 6" x 9" hardbound volumes
- Individual volumes, $39 each
- 200 pages per volume
- 10-12 profiles per volume — targets individuals within a specific subject area
- Contact sources for additional information
- Cumulative General, Places of Birth, and Birthday Indexes

NOTE: There is *no duplication of entries* between the **General Series** of *Biography Today* and the **Subject Series**.

Artists Series

VOLUME 1

Ansel Adams
Romare Bearden
Margaret Bourke-White
Alexander Calder
Marc Chagall
Helen Frankenthaler
Jasper Johns
Jacob Lawrence
Henry Moore
Grandma Moses
Louise Nevelson
Georgia O'Keeffe
Gordon Parks
I.M. Pei
Diego Rivera
Norman Rockwell
Andy Warhol
Frank Lloyd Wright

Author Series

VOLUME 1

Eric Carle
Alice Childress
Robert Cormier
Roald Dahl
Jim Davis
John Grisham
Virginia Hamilton
James Herriot
S.E. Hinton
M.E. Kerr
Stephen King
Joan Lowery Nixon
Gary Paulsen
Cynthia Rylant
Mildred D. Taylor
Kurt Vonnegut, Jr.
E.B. White
Paul Zindel

VOLUME 2

James Baldwin
Stan and Jan Berenstain
David Macaulay
Patricia MacLachlan

Scott O'Dell
Jerry Pinkney
Jack Prelutsky
Lynn Reid Banks
Faith Ringgold
J.D. Salinger
Charles Schulz
Maurice Sendak
P.L. Travers
Garth Williams

VOLUME 3

Candy Dawson Boyd
Ray Bradbury
Gwendolyn Brooks
Ralph W. Ellison
Louise Fitzhugh
Jean Craighead George
E.L. Konigsburg
C.S. Lewis
Fredrick L. McKissack
Patricia C. McKissack
Katherine Paterson
Anne Rice
Shel Silverstein
Laura Ingalls Wilder

VOLUME 4

Betsy Byars
Chris Carter
Caroline B. Cooney
Christopher Paul Curtis
Anne Frank
Robert Heinlein
Marguerite Henry
Lois Lowry
Melissa Mathison
Bill Peet
August Wilson

VOLUME 5

Sharon Creech
Michael Crichton
Karen Cushman
Tomie dePaola
Lorraine Hansberry
Karen Hesse
Brian Jacques
Gary Soto
Richard Wright
Laurence Yep

VOLUME 6

Lloyd Alexander
Paula Danziger
Nancy Farmer
Zora Neale Hurston
Shirley Jackson
Angela Johnson
Jon Krakauer
Leo Lionni
Francine Pascal
Louis Sachar
Kevin Williamson

VOLUME 7

William H. Armstrong
Patricia Reilly Giff
Langston Hughes
Stan Lee
Julius Lester
Robert Pinsky
Todd Strasser
Jacqueline Woodson
Patricia C. Wrede
Jane Yolen

VOLUME 8

Amelia Atwater-Rhodes
Barbara Cooney
Paul Laurence Dunbar
Ursula K. Le Guin
Farley Mowat
Naomi Shihab Nye
Daniel Pinkwater
Beatrix Potter
Ann Rinaldi

VOLUME 9

Robb Armstrong
Cherie Bennett
Bruce Coville
Rosa Guy
Harper Lee
Irene Gut Opdyke
Philip Pullman
Jon Scieszka
Amy Tan
Joss Whedon

VOLUME 10

David Almond
Joan Bauer
Kate DiCamillo
Jack Gantos
Aaron McGruder
Richard Peck

Andrea Davis Pinkney
Louise Rennison
David Small
Katie Tarbox

VOLUME 11

Laurie Halse Anderson
Bryan Collier
Margaret Peterson
  Haddix
Milton Meltzer
William Sleator
Sonya Sones
Genndy Tartakovsky
Wendelin Van Draanen
Ruth White

VOLUME 12

An Na
Claude Brown
Meg Cabot
Virginia Hamilton
Chuck Jones
Robert Lipsyte
Lillian Morrison
Linda Sue Park
Pam Muñoz Ryan
Lemony Snicket
  (Daniel Handler)

Scientists & Inventors Series

VOLUME 1

John Bardeen
Sylvia Earle
Dian Fossey
Jane Goodall
Bernadine Healy
Jack Horner
Mathilde Krim
Edwin Land
Louise & Mary Leakey
Rita Levi-Montalcini
J. Robert Oppenheimer
Albert Sabin
Carl Sagan
James D. Watson

VOLUME 2
Jane Brody
Seymour Cray
Paul Erdös
Walter Gilbert
Stephen Jay Gould
Shirley Ann Jackson
Raymond Kurzweil
Shannon Lucid
Margaret Mead
Garrett Morgan
Bill Nye
Eloy Rodriguez
An Wang

VOLUME 3
Luis W. Alvarez
Hans A. Bethe
Gro Harlem Brundtland
Mary S. Calderone
Ioana Dumitriu
Temple Grandin
John Langston
  Gwaltney
Bernard Harris
Jerome Lemelson
Susan Love
Ruth Patrick
Oliver Sacks
Richie Stachowski

VOLUME 4
David Attenborough
Robert Ballard
Ben Carson
Eileen Collins
Biruté Galdikas
Lonnie Johnson
Meg Lowman
Forrest Mars Sr.
Akio Morita
Janese Swanson

VOLUME 5
Steve Case
Douglas Engelbart
Shawn Fanning
Sarah Flannery
Bill Gates
Laura Groppe
Grace Murray Hopper
Steven Jobs
Rand and Robyn Miller
Shigeru Miyamoto
Steve Wozniak

VOLUME 6
Hazel Barton
Alexa Canady
Arthur Caplan
Francis Collins
Gertrude Elion
Henry Heimlich
David Ho
Kenneth Kamler
Lucy Spelman
Lydia Villa-Komaroff

VOLUME 7
Tim Berners-Lee
France Córdova
Anthony S. Fauci
Sue Hendrickson
Steve Irwin
John Forbes Nash, Jr.
Jerri Nielsen
Ryan Patterson
Nina Vasan
Gloria WilderBrathwaite

Sports Series
VOLUME 1
Hank Aaron
Kareem Abdul-Jabbar
Hassiba Boulmerka
Susan Butcher
Beth Daniel
Chris Evert
Ken Griffey, Jr.
Florence Griffith Joyner
Grant Hill
Greg LeMond
Pelé
Uta Pippig
Cal Ripken, Jr.
Arantxa Sanchez Vicario
Deion Sanders
Tiger Woods

VOLUME 2
Muhammad Ali
Donovan Bailey
Gail Devers
John Elway
Brett Favre
Mia Hamm
Anfernee "Penny"
  Hardaway
Martina Hingis
Gordie Howe
Jack Nicklaus
Richard Petty
Dot Richardson
Sheryl Swoopes
Steve Yzerman

VOLUME 3
Joe Dumars
Jim Harbaugh
Dominik Hasek
Michelle Kwan
Rebecca Lobo
Greg Maddux
Fatuma Roba
Jackie Robinson
John Stockton
Picabo Street
Pat Summitt
Amy Van Dyken

VOLUME 4
Wilt Chamberlain
Brandi Chastain
Derek Jeter
Karch Kiraly
Alex Lowe
Randy Moss
Se Ri Pak
Dawn Riley
Karen Smyers
Kurt Warner
Serena Williams

VOLUME 5
Vince Carter
Lindsay Davenport
Lisa Fernandez
Fu Mingxia
Jaromir Jagr
Marion Jones
Pedro Martinez
Warren Sapp
Jenny Thompson
Karrie Webb

VOLUME 6
Jennifer Capriati
Stacy Dragila
Kevin Garnett
Eddie George
Alex Rodriguez
Joe Sakic
Annika Sorenstam
Jackie Stiles
Tiger Woods
Aliy Zirkle

VOLUME 7
Tom Brady
Tara Dakides
Alison Dunlap
Sergio Garcia
Allen Iverson
Shirley Muldowney
Ty Murray
Patrick Roy
Tasha Schwikert

VOLUME 8
Simon Ammann
Shannon Bahrke
Kelly Clark
Vonetta Flowers
Cammi Granato
Chris Klug
Jonny Moseley
Apolo Ohno
Sylke Otto
Ryne Sanborn
Jim Shea, Jr.

World Leaders Series
VOLUME 1: Environmental Leaders 1
Edward Abbey
Renee Askins
David Brower
Rachel Carson
Marjory Stoneman
  Douglas
Dave Foreman
Lois Gibbs
Wangari Maathai

Chico Mendes
Russell A. Mittermeier
Margaret and Olaus J.
   Murie
Patsy Ruth Oliver
Roger Tory Peterson
Ken Saro-Wiwa
Paul Watson
Adam Werbach

VOLUME 2:
Modern African
Leaders

Mohammed Farah
   Aidid
Idi Amin
Hastings Kamuzu Banda
Haile Selassie
Hassan II
Kenneth Kaunda
Jomo Kenyatta
Winnie Mandela
Mobutu Sese Seko
Robert Mugabe
Kwame Nkrumah
Julius Kambarage
   Nyerere
Anwar Sadat
Jonas Savimbi
Léopold Sédar Senghor
William V. S. Tubman

VOLUME 3:
Environmental
Leaders 2

John Cronin
Dai Qing
Ka Hsaw Wa
Winona LaDuke
Aldo Leopold
Bernard Martin
Cynthia Moss
John Muir
Gaylord Nelson
Douglas Tompkins
Hazel Wolf